The Telling Quilt

Miranda Hathaway Adventure #13

Mary Devlin Lynch
and
Beth Devlin-Keune

This is a work of fiction. Names, characters, places, and incidents are the products of the authors' imaginations or are used fictitiously. Any resemblance to actual events, locales, or persons, living or dead, is entirely coincidental.

© 2024 Mary Devlin Lynch/Beth Devlin-Keune
All rights reserved
Published by *DevlinsBooks*

ISBN: 9798878877862

Dedication: The reason we continue these books is due to a small group of readers who ask, "When is the next book coming out?"
Thank you-- Nancy Stultz, Charlene Ferguson Heilberg, Maria Raus, Angela Robinson, and the many others.

This One's for you.

Contact Information:
 E-mail: devlinsbooks@gmail.com
 Facebook: devlinsbooks

One

"Miranda, are you ready?"

Jolted awake by my phone, I immediately regretted not turning it off last night. When I sleep, I sleep, thank you. Pulling it close, I squinted blearily at the time.

"It's 7:00, Queenie."

"I know. This is your wake-up call. You have half an hour to pull it together."

I blinked a few times. "For what?"

Queenie sighed impatiently. "The sale, don't you remember? Today is the sale at Edna Hammity's farm. You're going to help me get her quilts."

I pushed my hair out of my eyes. "Right. Today. Okay. But doesn't it start at 9?"

"Not for us, we are going to be the first ones through that door." She added impatiently, "I'll bring coffee and donuts, you get a move on."

"Okay." I did seem to remember agreeing to help her so I swung my legs out of bed. Normally, I'd have put on my comfy robe and meandered into the kitchen for my first cup. But not today. It was an estate sale emergency. That thought made me smile, just a little. Was there such a thing? Queenie certainly thought so.

Edna Hammity was a country quilter, one of the best in the county if not the state. She made her quilts the hard way, never buying fabric, using old jeans and shirts and anything else she could get for nothing. Her neighbors had taken to giving her their old stuff if the fabric looked interesting rather than toss it away. These were pieces not good enough for the charity shop, most of them with holes and stains. But if Edna could get a few squares or strips out of them, they were plenty good enough for her. She was a "waste not, want not" kind of quilter.

Some of her work reminded me of the Gee's Bend quilters who had come to the notice of the world a few years back. A small group of women from a remote community in Alabama had been creating amazing abstract quilts from anything, even feed sacks. They were a rare and wonderful example of passing down the useful yet joyous skill from generation to generation.

As I showered, I remembered what I knew about the sale and the Hammitys. It was likely that Emma, Edna and George's only daughter, was managing the sale. She had moved to the west coast some years ago but was back to help with the final arrangements.

It certainly wouldn't be George. The farm was his life and he expected it to be his wife and daughter's as well. Luckily for Emma, Edna was one of those quiet farm wives who never raised her voice but got it done anyway. Getting a college education for her daughter, for example. Once Emma had qualified for a couple of small scholarships, Edna had sold a few quilts to Queenie and neighbors, sold fresh flower bouquets from her own garden, made and sold jellies from berries she gathered, and pieced together enough to get the girl into the local community college.

I doubt that George ever knew how it had been done but I knew for sure he hadn't helped or approved. As far as he was concerned, Emma could either work the farm or marry another local farmer. While traditional roles are changing slowly, most farmers in our area still have several children, expecting one of them to take over the farm. I wondered briefly what would happen now that George was alone. If he was lucky, a cousin might step up. But I had no time to worry about it now.

Bathroom necessities completed, I threw on a pair of capris, a t-shirt, and sneakers, pulled my hair back into a ponytail, threw some moisturizer on, and grabbed my tote bag. I grabbed a fleece from the hall hook as a car horn blasted from the driveway.

As I quickly headed out, I opened the door to Gabe's office and said quickly, "Hey hon, headed out to an estate sale with Queenie."

Before he could respond, the horn sounded again. I grinned, "Apparently it's an emergency."

He grinned back. "Have fun."

I drew my brows together. "This is Queenie getting her hands on some quilts. It's not about fun, it's war." He laughed and I raced down the driveway before my friend could blow the horn again.

Two

True to her word, Queenie had two cups of coffee and a bag of donuts in the car. I took a few sips of the strong hot liquid and had a few bites of a Boston Creme before I spoke.

"So, it's about 20 minutes out to the farm, right?"

She nodded. "18 actually. We need to be there before 8."

I didn't bother to ask why. I knew as well as she did that Edna likely left a room full of quilts behind. If it was up to George, he'd probably have given them away; he had never valued Edna's work. We couldn't be sure how Emma would feel about them.

"You know..." I said between bites.

"Yes, I do. I always admired the way Edna managed to do her share of the farm work and still find time for her quilting."

I swallowed and nodded. "And she never let her sour-faced husband keep her from it."

"I still can't believe she was only 58. And yet the doc said her heart gave out, natural causes. Who dies of natural causes at 58?" Queenie paused, then answered her own question. "She didn't take care of herself, that's what. Too busy taking care of everybody else."

I nodded. She wasn't the only woman around here like that, the strong ones who were the centers of families, sometimes large families. These women never had the time to be sick or go to the doctor; they were too busy taking care of everyone else. We had posted signs in the Library encouraging annual physicals and mammograms. If Lucy or I saw someone looking at them, we didn't hesitate to engage them in a conversation in an effort to steer them towards self-care. I'd like to think we helped a few.

Edna had probably never spent much time on herself. I had certainly never run into her at a doctor's office. Yet, despite the demands on her time, despite her husband's general grumpiness, the small woman managed to work on her quilts. We had asked her to join our quilt guild but she shook her head with a smile and thanked us kindly.

"I would love too, ladies, I truly would, but I have to use my time wisely."

We understood. It wasn't hard to imagine the uproar it would have caused for her to leave the farm on Saturday mornings to do something that George considered frivolous. She already took off Sunday mornings for church, bringing gorgeous flowers from her little garden.

"At least..."

"He never kept her from going to church and bringing flowers." Queenie finished.

I giggled. "You're worse than Gabe, finishing my sentences. Apparently I've become..."

"Predictable." She replied with a chuckle.

I suppose that's true. Besides Queenie and Gabe, my best friend Dee always followed my train of thought. I expected it was because I was such a logical thinker. Librarian.

We pulled into the driveway and were, in fact, the first ones there for the sale or so it seemed. The only car in sight was a small blue Volvo, a little worn and a little rusty, parked over to one side. It sported a California plate.

"That would be Emma's," Queenie said quietly.

Her daughter had made most of the funeral arrangements and had given her mother a nice send off. It appeared that she had, as I had guessed, stayed to help her father let go of Edna's things. We sobered up. It was an estate sale. There were two goals: raise extra money but to also let go of things that belonged to a family member who no longer needed them.

Sometimes it made me sad, going through someone else's things, watching things they may have held dear being given away or sold for cheap. It was beyond me how folks could sometimes sell picture frames with the baby pictures or smiling wedding couples still in them. I steeled myself with the thought that any quilts Queenie bought would be valued and appreciated.

They had a nice day for the sale. It was May (Hurray, let's have a holiday). I smiled to myself.

Queenie laughed. "You're having a Camelot moment, aren't you?"

I might have pinked up a bit. "Maybe."

She sang, "Hurray, hurray, let's have a holiday."

I answered, "It's May, the lusty month of May, that lovely month when everyone goes blissfully astray..."

We nodded our agreement. There are some experiences that stick in your heart and mind. I know every word of the Camelot album and if I had a crush on Richard Harris, it was perfectly normal and understandable. He's been gone for a while now but even if you know him for MacArthur Park or as Dumbledore in the Harry Potter movies, he'll always be King Arthur to me. My mother played that album all through my formative years and we sang along until I became a teenager who would never have admitted to it. But it's a part of my happy memories, always. I will never deny Camelot, so there. Apparently, this is common knowledge among my friends.

Queenie and I sat sipping coffee and enjoying the serenity of the surroundings. The buds were opening, the sun was shining, the sky was a beautiful blue. It could have been a bit warmer for my taste but the sunny 60s was a decided improvement over the gloomy April 40s.

Even though it was clearly a working farm with green fields half planted, red barn with equipment parked in front, it also had that picture postcard feel to it. A couple of cows grazed contentedly in the field nearest the side of the house. George Hammity might be a tough man but he took pride in maintaining his property.

The front door opened and Emma stepped out. She was not a pretty girl as a teenager but moving away seemed to have done her good. I mentally calculated that she was now mid-30s and she had shaped herself into an attractive young woman. Her mother had done right by her, I thought, and I hoped she would remember that.

She walked toward the car.

"'Morning, ladies. You're a little early."

Queenie nodded. "I wanted to be the first to look at Edna's quilts," she said without apology.

The woman nodded. "You're the woman from the quilt shop in town, aren't you?"

"Yes." Queenie met her eyes firmly. "And I thought your mother made some wonderful things. I didn't want to miss out on a chance to buy them and find them new homes."

That brought a small smile to Emma's thin face. "She told me how kind you quilt ladies were to her. Why don't you come in, have a coffee with me, and I'll show you her quilts."

Queenie hesitated and looked around to make sure no one else was coming who might make a run for the house while she was having coffee but then nodded. "Thanks, Emma. That's very kind of you."

We got out of the car, Queenie introduced me, and we went inside. The kitchen was farmhouse old, not vintage or shabby chic, just shabby with old lino and a white metal sink and stove. The kitchen set was metal with what looked like contact paper on top in a floral pattern. The thought crossed my mind that anyone coming out to look for valuable antiques was in for a disappointment. On the other hand, the place was well-scrubbed and clean.

She poured us each a coffee into mismatched mugs and joined us, pushing aside some plates and bowls that were set out for the sale.

"So where do you live now, Emma?" Queenie asked politely as she sipped.

"LA." The woman answered with a smug look on her face. "I work in advertising."

"So you're just home to help your Dad."

She nodded but the look had gone a bit sour. For the first time, I saw the resemblance to George. "I'll leave after we get rid of most of Mom's stuff." She shrugged. "It's not like he's gonna do it. I'm taking a few mementos but it's," she waved a hand at the dishes, "mostly not my style."

I saw no harm in making my presence known. "Is he planning to stay in the house?"

Her eyes flickered over to me. "Not if I can help it. I'm trying to get him into that new development just outside of town, over by Mitchells'."

We nodded. We knew exactly where she meant.

"Millie Harticutt, another quilter and a friend of ours, donated the land for that." Queenie clarified.

"They're pretty nice places over there and the price is affordable if Dad will sell the farm." She sighed. "There are a couple of Amish families around that would pay cash."

Queenie and I exchanged glances. George selling the farm that had been in his family for probably over a hundred years? The phrase "over his dead body" came to me.

Emma chuckled. "If you could see your faces. I know. You're thinking, good luck with that." She shrugged. "But I owe it to Mom to try. He can't stay here by himself." She added, "You know, he's old school. Hardly knows how to make himself a cup of coffee or a meal, let alone do any housekeeping."

We nodded. That answered the question of whether any other relatives might be coming to the rescue. Still, we sure didn't envy Emma her task of moving George.

At that moment, the man himself appeared. Wearing bib overalls, work boots, and a scruffy gray beard, you would have known he was a farmer from a distance. I stifled a chuckle realizing it might also be from the smell his clothes exuded. He poured a cup of coffee, gave us a nod, and left.

When he had gone, Emma lowered her voice and leaned toward us. "Keep it to yourselves but I have an ace up my sleeve, you see. The Amish I've mentioned it to all agreed to let him keep working the farm for them. They offered to send a boy or two over so he can think he's doing them a favor by teaching them stuff." She winked. "It's all good."

There may have been a double sigh of relief and then all of us were smiling.

Three

True to her word, after she caught Queenie looking at her watch, Emma opened the door to a small bedroom and threw up the shades to let the light in.

These older farmhouses didn't have overhead lights and there was just one lamp which, of course, would only be turned on at bedtime. In the bright morning, we could easily see quilts stacked on the bed and on a couple of chairs.

Queenie's face lit up and I thought for a minute she was actually going to clap her hands together in glee. She moved over to examine a stack of bright quilts and I was right behind her.

But then Queenie stopped herself, turned to Emma and asked firmly, "How are you pricing these?"

The woman shrugged. "I was thinking $100 each. Does that seem fair?"

Without jumping up and down, to her credit, Queenie nodded. Emma left us to look. I walked around and put my hand on a few that spoke to me. I've always had a thing for Dresdens and found three that I really liked.

We heard a car door slam. Someone else had arrived!

Queenie quickly went out and found Emma. I could hear the conversation.

"We'll take the lot."

The woman's mouth fell open. "Really?"

Queenie nodded. "We'll take a count." She put out her red-tipped hand and Emma shook it with a smile.

"Done and done. Should I find some plastic bags or something?"

Queenie shook her head. "I brought my own boxes. Now, if you don't mind, I'm going to close the door to the room so no one else sees them and gets upset. When I get them out by the car, you can check the count and I'll pay you."

Emma hesitated. "Cash?"

"You betcha."

The young woman smiled in relief and nodded. "Excellent."

Queenie came back to me and asked me to run out to her car and bring in the cardboard boxes and tape while she folded and stacked. I was not surprised that she had taken them all. I also knew that she'd make sure I got the ones I wanted.

So I hustled outside and brought the boxes around to the back window while the Mission Impossible theme played in my head. Quietly as possible, we taped them up and folded the quilts inside while we heard voices of folks moving through the house. Queenie locked the door and I grinned at the thought of any poor soul who had opened it and tried to get between her and these quilts. There were 33 in all.

Queenie's face fell. "I only brought $3000 with me. I didn't realize there would be so many."

I pulled out my wallet and smiled. "It's meant to be. There are three I like and I have $330 in my wallet. We're good."

She blew out a sigh of relief that she didn't have to leave any behind or even make a quick trip to an ATM which might have given someone else a chance to get a few. Don't misunderstand, she's really a lovely, kind and generous woman. Except when it comes to quilting and quilts. Then it's gloves off.

She handed me the loaded boxes through the window and I moved quickly to place them on the other side of her car out of sight. I was a little concerned about getting them all inside her Honda. It sort of surprised me that she hadn't brought a larger vehicle but then I hadn't thought about that either.

As I was coming out with a box, I heard a shout. I was tempted to break into a run, escaping with the goods while I envisioned myself being chased by crazed quilt seekers with arms outstretched, when I recognized Judy, a member of our quilt guild and still owner of a mom mini-van. Without hesitating further, I raced over to her and handed her the box.

"We need help," I gasped. She opened her rear door and placed the box inside, then slammed it shut. She raced to the back of the house with me. She said a quick hello to Queenie through the window and grabbed another box. We trotted them out to her van. We ended up with four boxes in her van and three in Queenie's Honda.

Winded, I met Emma at Queenie's car and we opened each box and then went to Judy's to check those boxes.

"Should be 33," I panted.

She smiled. "I know I could have taken your word for it but I appreciate your showing me. Where's Queenie?"

I looked around. "Ohmigod. I think she must still be inside."

Judy, Emma and I hurried in to find Queenie examining some dishes in the kitchen. She looked up with a guilty grin.

"Queenie, Emma has counted the quilts. Time to pay up." I pulled $300 out of my wallet and handed it to Emma. Queenie opened her tote and pulled out a wad. She counted it into Emma's hand.

By now the place was filling up and I took Queenie by the arm and moved her toward the door. Judy gave us a wave and dove back in.

"Wow. That was awesome," I said when I had taken a good gulp of water in the car.

Queenie nodded. "Exactly the way I had hoped it would go. Do you want to come back and help me unpack and look at quilts?"

I looked at my watch; it was 10:00. "Or, while we wait for Judy to finish up here and drop off the rest, we could have a nice breakfast at the diner."

"Sounds good."

I sent Judy a quick text to let her know we were making a stop. She could leave the boxes in front of the shop or join us at the diner. It seemed the least we could do was treat her to breakfast or what was now becoming brunch.

"On my way!" She texted back with a happy face.

We had barely ordered when Judy slid into the booth.

I turned to her. "We didn't mean to rush you away."

She shrugged. "That's okay." Then she grinned. "I did make a good buy." She pulled a jewelry box out of her bag. Inside was a pair of earrings, gold dangles with red gemstones.

"Those are great," I said and Queenie nodded.

"I've wanted something new but I didn't feel like just going to the mall, you know?" She added, "I liked Edna."

We did. We understood that she had not just pretty earrings but a remembrance of a good woman.

"And now I'm getting breakfast! Life is good." Judy grinned.

After a hearty breakfast which did include bacon, we followed her van back to the store. Two hours later, the quilts were unpacked and stacked on Queenie's shop cutting tables. A couple of them were going to go to the dry cleaner but most were in good shape. I, however, was not.

"I think I need a nap." I yawned.

"Thanks for all your help, honey." Queenie replied with a smile and a hug. "I couldn't have done it without you."

I did not demur because I felt it was true since I had been the one hauling most of the boxes. I picked out the three quilts I had admired most and we were even as far as I was concerned. Then she reminded me I had bought breakfast and it devolved into silly talk about dollars and cents, or such nonsense, so I quickly picked up my quilts and went home.

When I got there, Gabe was gone. I'd have taken a bet that he was at Ryans' shop, working on birdhouses. Not just any birdhouses. The family had an internet business and local shop selling fun and unusual carved bird houses with fancy trim and colors. Some looked like homes for elves or fairies but they could also make you an exact replica of your own house to match for display in your front yard.

Queenie had a wonderful replica birdhouse of her family Victorian out front. Although I loved the concept, my standard ranch hadn't quite seemed like a good candidate for a replica. So I sported a little fairy house instead. It made me smile every time I saw it and seemed to be working out for a small finch family as well.

The Ryans' brick and mortar store had been a dusty, failing shoe store before Gabe found out about their father's secret skill and encouraged them to move it from a hobby to a moneymaker. Mr. Ryan, four of his five sons, and Gabe, were now engaged in profitable woodworking. (His oldest son, Max, was working in law enforcement out west).

Yes, my Gabe spends a lot of time with the Ryans. I don't mind. Gabe's first business after he retired as an FBI agent, was and is security and problem-solving for clients. Sometimes that involves wearing a gun; building birdhouses did not.

So I cuddled up in bed, read for a few minutes, and settled in for a luxurious Saturday afternoon nap. I was awakened by my husband.

"Everything okay, honey?"

I looked at my watch. It was after five. "Oh Lord, sorry, honey, I should have figured out dinner and I haven't given it a thought."

"No worries, I did realize you were having an estate sale emergency today." He replied wryly.

"Chinese?" I asked hopefully.

"Done."

"It's not easy being me." He sighed and hung his head, then clicked the number into his cellphone. "I'm underrated and unappreciated."

"What?" I jumped up and hugged him fiercely. "You are not."

He laughed. "And that is how you get your wife's attention."

I threw my pillow at him.

Four

Polly's phone rang and she didn't recognize the number so she didn't pick up. Several hours later, she checked her voice mail.

"Well, well, hit the jackpot, haven't we, Pol? You're probably gonna want to call me back before I decide just to drop in on you and dear old Aunt Millie for a little visit."

Polly closed her eyes. Damn it. She had figured this day would come but had been praying, just this once, she'd get a break. She texted back and agreed to meet him at a cafe in the next town over.

She needed to keep Michael as far away from Aunt Millie as possible for as long as she could.

Tears filled her eyes. Her good life where she was safe really had been too good to be true. Michael ruined everything he touched; he was selfish and mean.

Then the anger kicked in. He was going to ruin everything. She could just kill him.

Polly intended to do anything to keep him away from Aunt Millie. She would buy him off if she could but that had never worked before; he came back when he was broke again.

Her younger brother showing up was the worst that could happen. Polly comforted herself with the thought that she had never actually told Aunt Millie that she was an only child.

Five

Queenie was sorting through Edna's quilts, checking each one for damage or cleaning when she found the silk quilt.

She opened it completely across her quilt table, carefully examining it. Silk and embroidery. Without even looking again at the other quilts, she knew this was different. More than different, without being unkind, she was relatively sure that Edna Hammity had not made this quilt.

She called Miranda.

I answered with a flip, "Oh no, don't tell me we have another quilt emergency?"

Queenie chuckled. "Well, we have a quilt question but it's probably not an emergency. The thing is, I've been going through these quilts and there's one that's...different. I'd like you to take a look and see if you agree."

I looked at Gabe who shrugged. "Tell you what? We're having Chinese and there's enough for three. Would you like to bring it over here?"

"That's really sweet of you but I had a bite earlier. If you can spare a coffee, I'll be good."

"Done. See you."

When Queenie came in, Gabe got up, kissed the top of my head, and left us to it.

Queenie pulled the quilt out of the box and spread it across the table. Together, we checked for a tag or label. I even brought out my magnifying glass. On the back, in the lower right corner, I found it.

"Ah ha!" I said, doing my best Clouseau impression. "Mystery solv-ed." I handed the glass to Queenie who squinted at the close embroidered initials.

"EH." She hesitated. "Hummppphh."

"Edna Hammity. Maybe it was her secret masterpiece, the one she worked on in private and never let anyone else see," I suggested.

Queenie had been feeling the edges of the quilt and noticed a little extra thickness in the squares at the edges. I got my mini shears and she gently picked apart a seam.

A piece of paper fell out. It was yellow and fragile so I ran for my travel iron and we placed a thin towel over it and pressed it gently.

When we took the towel off, faded ink presented itself and we squinted to read it. Queenie pulled up the reading glasses that always hung on a chain around her neck.

April 22, 1962. I am to be married. Today is my 17th birthday. I don't like him.

We sat quietly for a moment. 1962? Edna was born in 1965; we had seen the Mass card. What was her mother's name? It took only a quick check on the local cemetery website to bring it up: Eleanor.

"Okay, so what we have here seems to be a quilt made by Edna's mother, Eleanor, into which she stuffed little diary papers?"

Queenie's bright red eyebrows were raised so I understood it was a genuine question.

I nodded. "Seems like. I have to say I've never seen anything like this before. We had that time when jewelry had been hidden in quilted hems and seams during colonial days to protect it but not paper diary pages."

"I remember. That was so cool." She grinned and added, "Diane will be so mad that she's not here."

"Yep."

My BFF Diane (Dee) and her husband Mark were on a much-delayed but much-needed vacation. Mark sold real estate and Dee taught high school English. Enough said. Their younger son, Ethan, was now a freshman in college; his older brother, Devon, a senior. So they took advantage of their empty nest and planned a getaway.

I couldn't remember the last time she had gone away without me. It seemed like most trips I took, she managed to invite herself along. I admit it felt weird not to see her every other day or so. We have had many adventures together and solved a few mysteries and everyone knows she totally hates to miss anything.

Gabe came in with the delivery bag in hand and, bless him, put out paper plates, napkins, and glasses of soda for us. We made sure to thank him profusely. As he slid into a chair next to me, I showed him the quilt and pointed at the small paper, afraid to pick it up.

"You guys just can't do ordinary, can you?"

"Hey, we didn't do anything," I responded warmly. "Queenie just bought a bunch of quilts from an estate sale and found this one in it."

"I know, honey. You just attract mystery." He squeezed my shoulder. "So what are you going to do with it?"

We looked at each other.

"There are more in there." Queenie pointed. "It's not just the one."

"We need to call Emma." I said firmly. "This is a family heirloom and we need to give it back."

I'm not gonna lie, my first instinct was to want to get it away from me. I, we, had no right to be reading these family secrets.

"You're right." Queenie's face echoed my thoughts.

Neither of us had Emma's cell number so we called the home phone line for the house. No one answered. I could just see Arthur sitting there, letting it ring, the stubborn old goat.

We did give it some thought but couldn't think of any close friends that she might have here.

Finally, in desperation, we called the funeral home and got her number from the receptionist who happened to be someone I went to high school with. I knew, the whole time, that Diane would have done this better and faster. At any rate, we bumbled through some cockamamie explanation as to why we needed it and Paula didn't see the harm in giving it to me. I guess funeral homes don't have a great need for confidentiality policies.

Queenie dialed while Gabe and I listened in. Emma didn't pick up so she left a message.

"Hey Emma, this is Queenie McQueen. I bought your mom's quilts this morning. I think there's one here you really should see and that you might want back. I'll be at the shop tomorrow after 10 if you'd like to stop by or just give me a call and we'll set something up. Thanks." Click.

Well, that was a relief. So we had coffee and dug some teaberry ice cream out of the freezer for dessert. Teaberry ice cream is probably just a Pennsylvania thing like Lebanon bologna. I can only describe the taste for you this way. Have you ever tasted one of those little silver balls that you use for decorating cookies? That's the flavor. Other than that, it's pink and it tastes pink. Try it if you can find it!

My preoccupation with food aside, my last thoughts of the day centered on this quilt. My natural curiosity about what might be hidden inside the quilt was quite overwhelmed by my feeling that we needed to get this back to Eleanor's granddaughter.

Six

"I'm not giving the money back."

When Queenie called me the next morning, that's the first thing she told me that Emma had said to her. But she had agreed to stop by the shop around noon.

Just to be polite, I asked Queenie if she wanted me there. Maybe I had harbored some small hope she'd say 'no.' But no such luck.

So after Gabe and I had a lovely omelet together, he went off to read the Sunday paper while I drove into town.

She was late but I didn't mind because there seemed to be some fabrics I hadn't seen before. My tastes are pretty eclectic. I love Riley Blake and her tinies as much as I love the wild and crazy designs of Kaffe Fassett. We should have had our weekly Cutler Quilt Guild #1 meeting yesterday but Queenie had called it in favor of the estate sale and we all understood.

When the cheery little bell rang, announcing the arrival of our visitor, we both looked up and then moved to the cutting table where the quilt lay folded.

"I hope this won't take long. I've got a lot to do." Emma said brusquely.

"It won't," I answered. So far, Queenie had been patient with the woman's rudeness but I knew it couldn't last long.

Silently, Queenie pulled the lid off and took out the quilt.

"So?" Emma shrugged. "Look, if you don't want it, give it away."

"Please listen, honey. This is not your mother's work," I put in. "We think it was your grandmother's."

"Oh." She came closer and touched it. "Okay. Well, it was nice of you to let me know."

"Wait. That's not the headline here," Queenie said quickly to keep Emma from racing out the door. She took out the delicate paper we had found. "It seems that your grandmother used the quilt as sort of a diary. I guess she didn't trust her secrets to be safe anywhere else."

Now we had her attention. She read the slip and swallowed.

"My grandmother died before I was born. She was pretty young, I think."

Queenie rubbed another edging square between her fingers. "The thing is that there seem to be more of these in the edging of the quilt. We felt that it ought to be your call as to whether to take them out or not." She added, "Or you can just take it with you and decide in your own time."

Her shoulders fell. "I see." She closed her eyes for a minute. "I've just got a lot going on right now. Can I think about it?"

"Of course. Are you sure you don't want to take it home with you?"

She shook her head vehemently. "God, no. I'm trying to deal with Dad and seeing a quilt coming back to the house might send him into one of his tempers. Do you mind holding on to it?"

"No problem."

Queenie had a thought, then a question. "Emma, what was your grandmother's last name?"

"Hold on, let me think. Harmon. That's it, I'm sure."

Queenie and I exchanged relieved looked. EH stood for Eleanor Harmon. One mystery solved.

Watching our faces, Emma said in a softer tone, "I can give you your money back on it."

Queenie smiled for the first time. "Don't be silly. I got the rest for a good price. This is a family heirloom. It belongs to you if you want it." She added gently, "Diary entries and all."

I saw Emma swallow as she nodded. I had a sudden sense that she was not used to or expecting kindness. It gave me pause to wonder what her life had really been like away from here. And what had happened to her that she had come to expect so much less.

Seven

It wasn't easy waiting for Emma to make up her mind. Fortunately, both Queenie and I were busy with our real lives.

In addition to being Head Librarian at the Cutler Library, I spend a fair amount of time either video chatting with my new triplet grandbabies and my daughter or in my sewing room making up special items for them.

Of course, I manage to work in some quality time with Gabe as he juggles his investigations and woodworking.

We manage dinner together almost every night and then play Jeopardy with Harry. Each of the three of us has our own recliner. Yes, Harry is our cat and an active player. When he knows an answer, he mutters it in Catish and we applaud him and give him the point. We have to be pretty sincere about it or his eyes narrow suspiciously.

I find it's about the categories really. If it comes to Geography or Capital Cities, Gabe has an advantage because he traveled the world as an FBI agent. If English Literature or Authors come up, well, I am a Librarian! Harry enjoys the Animal categories especially if there are picture clues.

It's a fairly simple and quiet life, mostly, but over time, we have had more than a few adventures, many of which involved Dee, who considers herself Watson to my Sherlock.

I know how lucky I am to have had the same best friend since first grade and to have lived in the same town my whole life. I don't have the constitution to be a world traveler; I realized that early on. At this point, I have been a few places, even to Paris once (fabulous!), but I sure know people who have never left the state. I can't say that they seem much the worse for it.

Queenie, of course, had a quilt shop to run. She had one part-timer who filled in over lunch and when she had appointments or such. Other than that, she was a one-woman show. I was constantly amazed by her ability to do the bookkeeping, ordering, work with customers, and manage to do some custom quilting. Then there is Cutler Quilt Guild #1 of which she is President. She handles requests from charities, runs our meetings, sets up for projects, and even makes sure we have snacks for our break.

We both had a couple of days to get back to normal and absorb what we had found out already before Emma called Queenie. Queenie then called me at the Library and paraphrased the call for me. What Emma said came out something like this...

"So, I am going to ask you ladies a favor. Would you mind taking out the papers and looking at them? Just to let me know if there's anything that's...going to be hard for me to see or going to impact my life in any way?"

My heart sank. "My Lord, what did you say?"

She sighed. "To be honest, I was so stricken I didn't answer right away. So then she got all defensive and said she knew it was a lot to ask."

I nodded, even though I knew she couldn't see me through the phone. "You know, it really is. She's asking you to make a judgment call on her personal family history. It's not really fair."

"You're not wrong."

"But, of course, you said you'd do it."

"Me? You mean us, right? You are going to do this with me, right?"

I didn't want to, really. I wasn't the one who bought the darn quilt and I wasn't the one who found the first paper. I wasn't even the one Emma called. But there wasn't really a choice. As if my guilty conscience would ever let me abandon Queenie to do this alone.

"Okay." I'm sure my lack of enthusiasm was palpable.

"Do you want to come to the shop?"

"Sure. I'll go home, change, grab a bite, and come over."

The shop would be closed so if we did this in Queenie's office in the back, we could avoid any passing neighbors pounding on the door or calling the police to report a light on in the shop. Yep, that's what it's like in a small town, for better or worse.

I let Gabe know and he agreed to have a salad ready for me. No point in bothering with a full meal, I had sort of already lost my appetite. Diane would have made this sound like an adventure, crowing that maybe we'd discover directions to a hidden treasure. I smiled to myself envisioning her face, her brown eyes glowing, her curls bouncing. She usually had enough enthusiasm for both of us.

But she wasn't with me when I knocked on the door of Queenie's shop. The bell that rang gaily as I walked in didn't reflect my mood.

Queenie gave me a bottle of water and I followed her to the back. Then she handed me a seam ripper. For a moment, I recalled again the quilt ripper adventure, when we had discovered hidden jewelry in quilted items. Now, I had to admit, that was fun. I had a feeling this was not going to be.

We spread the quilt over her desk and she started down one side and I started down the other. We realized at once that each entry was dated and started stacking them so we could read them in chronological order.

It went quicker than we expected. After we had gone round the edges, we felt the rest of the quilt to be sure there weren't more.

We ended up with a stack of about twenty slips. It didn't seem like enough to document a life. We smoothed them out gently and pressed them as we had the first one.

Queenie started reading them out loud.

"You'll remember that the first one said Eleanor was going to be married and she was 17."

I nodded and took a drink of water. We both knew that farm families needed to marry off their daughters to gain land, animals, and connections. There was no use pretending it didn't happen then and that it doesn't happen now. The boys were allowed more freedom although they were

expected, too, to marry in some way that benefitted the family.
Queenie placed a small "2" in the corner of the next slip.

(2) *July 10, 1962. My wedding day. His name is Harold. He's twice my age and smells like manure. I should have run away.*

We breathed out at the same time, feeling sorry for the girl.
Queenie had an odd look on her face (which is very expressive normally).
"What?" I asked, somewhat concerned.
"You know, my Mom said my grandmother married at 15. It never occurred to me to wonder if she loved my grandfather. They were together for over 50 years. I don't think it would ever have occurred to her to divorce him, no matter what."
I grinned at her. "Not sure divorce was much of a thing back in the 1800s."
She gave me a fake glare. "Ha ha."
I thought it time to move on. I never knew my grandparents, any of them. Having discovered that I was adopted, I would have had two sets on each side. My mother (in Pennsylvania, who raised me) had told me her mother died during a flu outbreak. Her father had died of a heart attack. This had all happened when I was a baby. I guess it was odd if I thought about it. No one had ever mentioned my

father's parents. My birth mother's parents were gone, I knew. I honestly couldn't remember my sister Meredith saying anything about our father's parents at all. Why hadn't I asked?

"I'm sorry," Queenie said quietly. "Didn't mean to bring up old history."

"Well, that's what we're doing, isn't it?" I replied with a shrug. "We have to decide how much we need to know about ours but now we have to live with Emma Hammity's as well."

"I know I got you into this and I feel bad about that now. But let's push through, okay?"

"Okay." I took a swig of water, pushed all thoughts of my own past aside, and listened.

(3) *September 2, 1962. So this is married life. I work from dawn until dusk. He expects a lot. If I'm lucky, he falls asleep fast…*

"Geez, not much of an intro to sex, was it?" Queenie muttered.

For just that moment, it was too easy for us to imagine ourselves, young and scared, being tackled by a smelly guy who had never met the word 'romance' and cared less about our engagement in the process.

"Poor kid." I said with feeling.

(4) *March 6, 1963. He is angry that I'm not pregnant. He is angry because I don't do more to please him in bed. I cry* because I don't know how and it's hard when he's so mean. I tried to talk to Mom but she doesn't want to hear it.*

It was Queenie's turn to stop and take a drink of water and a breath before continuing.

(5) *June 15, 1963. I figured out how to do this now. He has shown me what he wants. I am so sweet to him that he doesn't hit me as much. But I have taken steps to protect myself.*

"Wait, what?" I looked at my friend, wide-eyed. "What does that mean?"
Queenie shrugged. "Either she got hold of some birth control or she got hold of a gun."
"Ohmigod. Do you really think?"

(6) *April 17, 1964. My 19th birthday. Today I met someone in town who smiled at me and made me feel pretty. I made myself a small cake.*

"Oh no. This can't be good." I murmured and Queenie nodded.
"Especially not since her husband seems like a "shoot first" kind of guy," she added.

(7) *September 4, 1964. I am pregnant at last. The bastard thinks it's his.*

I closed my eyes. This was exactly what I had feared-a family secret that was now no longer secret. Heaven only knew what kind of damage it could do out in the open even if those directly involved were dead and gone.

Queenie cleared her throat. "Okay, so we know that Eleanor is pregnant."

"And we can't un-know that it's not her husband's."

"Well, she didn't say that for sure." Queenie hedged. "I'm pretty sure she wouldn't have done a test or anything."

I stared at her. "She all but said she was using birth control with him."

"Maybe it got so she figured it was safer to stop using it than to keep making him mad."

"Enough," I waved a hand. "I need a break."

Queenie agreed. "Yes, and I need…"

"Pie?"

She laughed. "Exactly. Why don't I go over to the bakery before they close and meet you at your house?"

"Excellent."

We moved quickly (the bakery closes at 8). I hurried home and made some fresh coffee. After Queenie showed up with an apple pie, Gabe came into the kitchen, sniffing.

"Wow, pie. As bad as all that, girls?" He threw me a mischievous look. "There might be some vanilla ice cream in the freezer."

I pecked him on the cheek. "Okay, you can have some pie."

He whispered into my ear. "Harry is in a snit because you missed Jeopardy without telling him. He didn't want to hear it from me."

That's when I realized that I hadn't seen Harry since I got home. He usually meets me at the door or, at this time of night, should have been trying to convince me that no one had given him supper, draping himself pathetically over his empty bowl.

"Give me a minute."

I went into the living room. Harry was still in his recliner, head on paws. I sat down in my own chair next to him. "I'm sorry, sweetie. But something came up. We're sort of solving a mystery."

He didn't raise his head but his eyes moved toward me so I knew he was listening.

"I am so sorry that I missed our family time, I know I've been away a lot but I will make it up to you"

I stroked his back. "It's okay, love."

After a few minutes, he jumped down and left the room. Not the way he leaves with his tail held high in disgust but with his tail down as if he didn't have the energy to hold it up.

"Well, this is new," Gabe said, puzzled.

I stood up and went out to the kitchen table where my warm apple pie topped with ice cream and a fresh coffee awaited.

Gabe sat down to eat with us so we filled him in on what we knew so far.

"So Eleanor was seemingly forced to marry a guy twice her age, which, weirdly, would really only make him 34 but I guess it seemed older then. He was hard on her, both sexually and physically. He hit her. We think she was getting him back by not getting pregnant, when she knew he really wanted kids. Then she met someone else and did get pregnant. She seems pretty sure it's not her husband's baby. That's it so far."

"Good God. And you're what, about half way through?"

We nodded.

"And Emma expects you to decide how much of this to tell her?"

We nodded again.

He picked up his pie, grabbed his coffee, and headed toward his office. "Sucks to be you," he muttered on his way out.

"I heard that," I called after him.

"I know," he called back.

I envied Gabe and wondered briefly if running after him and closing myself in the office was an option for me. But I saw the same look on Queenie's face that I knew was on my own. It's hard not being a quitter.

Okay, we had interfered in other people's business before, fair enough. But there was always a reason, an upside. Maybe they were criminals and needed to be caught. Maybe there was something owed to them that needed to be returned. This seemed simply gratuitous somehow. What good would come of it?

"It feels like…"

"We're eavesdropping in someone's bedroom," Queenie finished in a tired voice. "This is none of our business."

"Right."

"I say we sleep on it and decide tomorrow whether to continue with this."

I yawned and nodded my agreement. We'd certainly had enough for one day.

Lying in bed later next to my softly snoring husband, I tried to spin this situation. Maybe there was a happy ending buried in the rest of the notes.

Yeah, right.

Eight

Polly looked around the cafe carefully to make sure there was no one there that she knew or who might recognize her. She was also wearing a ball cap and sunglasses. As she slid into the booth she took off the glasses and looked at the man across from her.

Michael was one of those men who would always be good looking, boyish good looks eventually changing into distinguished charm. He grinned at her but she saw the shadows under his eyes. She didn't smile back.

The waitress came over and he ordered a BLT and coffee while Polly just asked for an iced tea. She knew that she would be sick if she tried to eat.

As soon as their orders arrived and the waitress left, she made a move to get this over with.

"What do you want?"

"Nice to see you too, sis."

"It's never nice to see you, Michael. You only ever appear when you want something. How did you find me?"

His smile faded. "I have friends, that's how. I'm truly disappointed that you're not glad to see me." He leaned toward her. "I've been watching this sweet set up you have going with the old lady."

Polly paled. "You go near her and I'll…"

He shrugged. "Hey, I'm as much a Harticutt as you are, the way I see it. Maybe she'd be thrilled to have a male heir turn up." His eyes narrowed. "I could even have kids and continue the family line, right? Wouldn't that be something?"

Polly wanted to cry but she willed the tears back. "What will it take for you to go back to where you came from?"

Michael munched on his sandwich and took a drink of his coffee. "The thing is that I owe some money to some bad guys who can find me like I found you. I need to either pay up or go far away."

"How much?"

"I owe 25 so 50 would be good, give me enough to start over."

"$2500?"

He chuckled. "Oh, darlin'. $25,000."

Polly gasped. "I don't have that kind of money."

"No, but she does."

"Oh Michael, if I were to ask Millie for that kind of money, I'd have to explain. It will ruin everything."

His face hardened. "Not for me. So you think about it this way. Either you come up with at least $35 large and I go away OR I can come home with you now and introduce myself."

The thought of Michael in the house with her and Millie was almost too much to bear thinking about. Polly swallowed. "I need time to think about it."

"Okay, that's fair. Give me a bit of cash to hold me over and I'll give you three days." He finished his sandwich in a couple of large bites and drained his coffee. He looked at her with hard eyes. "Gotta take care of number one, baby."

Polly had known better than to come with an empty purse. She pulled out $300 and handed it to him.

He looked at her hard, then jammed it into his pocket.

"If you don't call me by 5 o'clock on Wednesday, I'll be knocking at your door." As he slid out of the booth, he said lightly, "You look good."

Of course he left her with the bill, Polly thought. Of course he did.

She closed her eyes for a minute or two, forcing herself to accept that he was here. She certainly did need time to think about how to get rid of him, hopefully without Millie ever knowing.

The waitress came over to clear and said softly, "That's a bad seed right there, honey." She put a warm hand on Polly's shoulder. "I hope you sent him on his way."

Polly, startled, looked up into the worn, kindly face.

"I'm trying."

The waitress nodded her approval, then said in a low voice as she picked up the check and $20 bill from the table. "Try harder."

Nine

Thursday morning came and I went to work. I put the entire Eleanor thing out of my mind, almost. I had a lot of other things to think about—and apparently some I had forgotten.

Lucy popped her head in and grinned at me.

"You look like you're puzzling a puzzle with your puzzler."

That brought out a smile. "I've thunk and I've thunk till my thinker is sore."

We are both Dr. Seuss fans so these odd exchanges happen more often than you would think.

She gave me an appreciative chuckle. "Anything I can help with?"

"I wish. No, it's simply something I'm helping Queenie with that I sort of wish I hadn't gotten into. One of those situations where you thought-how bad can it be?"

"Right. Bummer. So we're supposed to cull the children's books today."

"Okay." I don't like doing that and she knows it. It calls for making some tough choices. Every time I pull a book off the shelves, I imagine some little person frantically looking for that very book. It's like discarding old family photos.

"Or…" She dragged it out dramatically. "I could do that while you organize the rest of the book sale for Saturday."

I swallowed. "Oh Lord, I haven't done a thing, have I?"

"It's okay, there's time. It's not like we haven't done it before." She added, "The signs are already up and the buzz has started."

"I'm on it."

I opened my laptop and pulled up the sales file. Thank heaven, after the first few sales where there may have been a few missteps, we had made lists of everything that needed to be done. Now either of us, or anyone else who could read for that matter, could walk through the process.

The goal was to rid the library of books that were least popular when the shelves started overflowing. We put boxes into the back room and, when we had enough, we offered them up at $5 a bag. We found that it was better if we provided the brown bags from the market after several ingenious types showed up with huge black trash bags. So calling the market for bags was on the list.

We don't make a lot but it truly is fun. It serves several purposes beyond the culling. Our little community turns out in force. It is rare to see books causing this kind of excitement and we know that. It's a joy to see the little ones clutching a book in their arms. It's heartwarming to see families who don't have much walking out with a bag of books and big smiles. You don't have to have an internet connection to read a book.

As a small community library, we see ourselves as more than just bookshelves, also as a meeting place, and that keeps the place open and the community council from reducing our budget below functioning level.

We have Friday evening gatherings and book signings and children's story hours. We take every suggestion made by our users seriously, except the silly ones, of course, like the request for a couple of big screen TVs.

By lunchtime Thursday, I was feeling good about the sale. We would work late Friday, physically setting up, but I had lined up extra hands to help and all the little boxes were ticked off.

Lucy and I grabbed sandwiches and ate in our breakroom. It was always a pleasure for me to see the small diamond sparkling on her finger. Jimmy Haynes, our chief of police and her fiancé, had gone through a hard year. Cutler wasn't the safe haven it had once been when his job entailed parking tickets and Saturday night drinkers sleeping it off in the cells.

Now, it was like anywhere else with drugs, robberies, beatings, and murder. The fire which destroyed a good part of the Cutler Candy factory had also taken the life of the night watchman. Since then, Jimmy's job involved real crime solving now.

Happily, Taylor Perryman, the wife of the previous chief, had been keeping an eye on him and recognized the need to change our police department. She was the first to realize that Jimmy was exhausted and stretched too thin. After all, her husband Jake had died of a heart attack on the job dealing with his first serious case.

We all knew that. So when Taylor came to speak to the Quilt Guild and asked for our help, we fell into line. We took up the cause and obtained some funding (mostly from Millie Harticutt) to get Jimmy some more officers, cars, and training. He now had two days off each week when things were quiet. They were quiet now and we could only pray it stayed that way. He and Lucy were making plans for their wedding.

After lunch, I helped Lucy box up the children's books for the sale.

At five, I waved goodbye to our desk volunteers and headed home. Gabe had made us lasagna for dinner. I'm a lucky woman and I know it. Having been distracted a bit lately, I gave him a big hug and kiss before we ate.

He smiled. "So it's lasagna, is it? You know I could make and freeze a couple of batches…"

I smiled back. "That would be lovely." I was relaxed after a hot meal and a glass of wine. Then the phone rang.

"So are we doing this or what?" Queenie demanded.

I looked at the clock. It was almost time for Jeopardy.

"I don't suppose we could wait until tomorrow night?" I asked hopefully.

"Fine." She answered in a tone that said it wasn't.

I blew out a breath. "Are you at home or the shop?"

"Shop."

"I'll be over in a few minutes."

Gabe was clearly disappointed and so was I.

"I'm sorry, honey." It was seven o'clock and Harry appeared in the doorway.

"JJassshhhhheeee." He yelled.

We are always amazed that either we understand Catish better all the time or he's actually learning English.

I went over and stroked his head. "I'm sorry, sweetie, I have to go out."

His eyes narrowed, then went to Gabe.

My tolerant husband stood up. "Okay, I'll play, Harry. But then I have to do the dishes."

Without comment, the cat returned to the living room, jumped up on his recliner and waited.

Gabe gave me a quick hug. "At least you're not doing anything dangerous."

"I will be back." I whispered in his ear seductively.

His eyes lit up. "And I'll be here."

We heard an impatient snort from the living room. Harry hates missing the beginning of the show when they introduce the players.

I find that I realize how much I enjoy my everyday life mostly when it gets disrupted.

As soon as I stepped inside, Queenie waved me into her office.

"Let's get it over with," she said.

"Agreed."

She pulled out the pile of fragile slips and picked up #8.

(8) Christmas, 1965. BH has gone. I wonder if I should have told him about the baby.

"Oh for the love of God. BH? How are we supposed to figure out who that is?" I said in exasperation.

Queenie was subdued. "Maybe we're not supposed to."

I waved a hand. "Let's keep going. Maybe she'll drop another hint."

(9) *June 17, 1965. It's a girl. I'm so happy. Harold wanted a boy so bad. I named her Edna after my mom, too.*

"She's not going to mention the father again, is she?"
Queenie shook her head.

(10) *May 14, 1966. I had a miscarriage. It was a boy. The doctor says I'm unlikely to have another baby. I almost feel sorry for Harold-almost.*

I felt sorry for both of them, really. She was still so young. I mean, what is she, like 21?"

Queenie checked the notes. "Yep."

I shook my head. "Unbelievable."

"Different times."

"Thank God."

(11) *January 12, 1968. I came home from the store and found a red mark on Edna's face. She was hiding under her bed. I found Harold in the barn. He said she talked back. That's once. He hits me, I'm used to it. But not my baby.*

"I don't like the sound of this."

"This is not going to end well," Queenie echoed.

(12) February 22, 1968. He hit her again. I was right there. So last night, I woke him and showed him the baseball bat in my hand. "You ever touch her again, I will kill you in your sleep."

My phone rang and we both jumped. I waved a 'give me a minute' finger at Queenie.

"Dee!"

"I'm baaacccckkkk." She crowed.

"I missed you."

"Of course you did."

"What did I miss?"

"Tell you what? Can you do lunch tomorrow at Sylvia's? I'll bring you up to speed."

"Ooh, sounds exciting. I'm only letting you off the hook tonight because I am a bit travel weary."

"Understood. See you tomorrow. One o'clock."

After I hung up, Queenie looked at me.

"Are you sure you want to bring Diane into this?"

"No. But I also know that if anyone can figure out who this BH is, it's her. I'll swear her to secrecy."

"Okay." She looked at me with concern. Diane is not known for her discretion. "We don't want this getting all over town before we've discussed it with Emma."

"I know. I'll try to give her just the pertinent facts and asked her to find BH."

"Good."

Queenie had been tapping on her phone while I was talking to Dee.

"What are you doing?" I pointed.

She swallowed. "I was curious about something." She hesitated. "Harold Hammity died in June of 1968. Farm accident."

We sat in silence for a minute. Farms are generally isolated places and accidents happen. We knew a farmer who had lost most of his foot trying to loosen a stuck combine and almost bled out before help came. It is dangerous work and often work done alone. It's easy to make a death look like an accident.

"Wow, this just gets better and better. Emma's grandfather…" No need to finish.

"It was about four months later, probably an accident." Queenie shrugged. "And if Eleanor didn't rush out to get help, well, I'm not sure I'd blame her."

I was quiet for a minute. "We're in no position to make a judgment."

The day's surprises were not over. When I checked my phone, I found a message from my sister in Virginia. We had only met a couple of years ago. By now, we had worked through our initial shock at finding out we had been triplets and the two of us were adopted out. We were crafting a working relationship. I had invited her to join us for Christmas and she had come. Since her parents were still alive and she lived with them at a horse farm, she came between the holiday and New Years and that was fine with me.

It was odd to hear from her in the middle of the summer. I left it to call back later.

Queenie and I agreed that we had lost interest for the day.

"Of course I'll let you know what Dee comes up with," I said as I stood. "I have the book sale at work so I may have to let you know when I can come back to finish up."

"That's fine. Friday and Saturday are busy for me, too." She grinned. "It's not like we're avoiding it or anything."

"Of course not."

Ten

"Merrie!"

"Miranda!"

This is the way we usually began our conversations. It quickly broke the ice and re-established our connection.

"How are you?"

"Good. You?"

"Good." Merrie hesitated. "I have something to tell you. Are you sitting down?"

It had already been a long day, truth be told, so I was sitting down. "Oh my, is this bad news?"

"Uh, no. It's just going to be a bit of a surprise and I'm hoping not too much of a shock."

I sighed. "Okay, rip off the bandage."

I heard her take a breath. "Rose called me."

"Rose?"

"Our sister. The one that was missing is no longer missing."

I felt faint. Finding a sister had taken some getting used to. We had both reconciled ourselves to the fact that our third triplet sister was gone. I had found no way to trace her when I went south.

"Are you still there?"

"Mostly." I swallowed. "How? When?"

"She called me about a week ago." She paused. "Do you remember when you went south and met that woman in that basement place?"

How could I forget? "Sure. Her name was Jane Harris."

"Well, the reason she gave you the brush off about the third baby was that she kept it and raised her as her own. She never told Rose and thought that Rose never knew about her mother or us. But she did." She paused for breath. "Are you with me?"

I nodded and then realized she couldn't see me. "I'm with you."

"Okay, so Jane passed away about a month ago so Rose felt free for the first time to reach out. She didn't want to do it while Jane was alive. She didn't want to hurt her."

I struggled to keep up. "My God."

"I know." She hesitated. "She'd like to meet you."

Another sister. Growing up as an only child, I had gotten used to my solitary state, except for Diane, of course, who was as close to a sister as I could have imagined.

"To be honest, Merrie, it's been a long day. Can I think about it?"

"Of course. I feel the same way. I'll talk to her on the phone a bit and see how it goes." She chuckled. "Now you have time to adjust."

"Thanks, Merrie."

My head was spinning. The thought occurred that my horoscope for this week must have been a doozy.

Even my usually unflappable husband was stunned by this news. But one of his many admirable qualities is that he doesn't push me. He listens.

I babbled. "So this is a good thing, right? I mean, best of all possible outcomes? We're all still around and have a chance to get to know each other. It's all good, right?" I looked into his crystal blue eyes. He knew better than to answer.

He sighed and held my hand and his warmth flowed through me. We both knew I had to decide whether I wanted to meet Rose even as we both knew it wasn't really a choice at all, any more than meeting Merrie had been. So why did I feel like crying?

Eleven

"So what did I miss?" Dee said without preamble.

I popped up from the booth and hugged her. Upon closer inspection, she looked tired for someone who had gone on vacation. "Are you okay?"

She grinned. "Sure, just had all the fun I could stand. Had to come home to get a rest." She winked at me.

"So where did you go? What was the big mystery?"

"New York City! We had Broadway show tickets! It was awesome."

I relaxed. I guess we've all done that, taken what was supposed to be a break and turned it into a fast-paced, see all you can see situation.

"Well, you might want to order first." I wiggled my eyebrows. "We did have a bit of excitement."

"I knew it! I told Mark something was going on, my Spidey sense was tingling."

Sylvia approached. "Ladies, we have chili with corn bread or hot dogs with sauerkraut and homemade chips."

She looked at Dee, then me. "Okay, two chilis then. And two iced teas." She gave Dee another glance. "You been out of town?"

Dee nodded. "Yep, went to New York."

"Ah, trying out for the Rockettes again?"

Dee sat a little straighter. "Nah, been there done that."

To our surprise, Sylvia laughed and punched her in the shoulder.

I felt my eyes widen.

Dee leaned toward me. "Has there been a change in the force while I was gone?"

"Wow. Maybe she missed you, too."

"Okay, we'll go with that."

Sylvia brought our iced teas without comment. There was no doubt that things had changed over the past year. When the candy factory blew up, her husband Charley had been close to retirement. There were a few weeks of uncertainty. Would he get his pension? But the family that owned the factory had come through and agreed to pay all benefits. They were still working on converting it to a water bottling plant but had offered early retirement or help with other employment to any of the former workers who didn't want to make the change.

As far as I knew, Charley was working there. He had always struck me as one of those guys who thinks he's working toward retirement but has no idea what he's gonna do when he gets there. Still, all that uncertainty had taken its toll on many in our small community. We had surely seen the worry on Sylvia's face during that time. It was a relief to see her back to her usual self.

Our lunch appeared and we dug in. Sylvia makes the best meatloaf in town, possibly in the world, but her chili is right up there, too. I swear, she could give me the list of ingredients and mine still would never come close.

After we'd each had a few bites, I cleared my throat. She smiled. "Spill."

"I can't tell you everything just yet. Someone else needs to be told first, it's personal. But I could use your help. We need to find a guy who left town in the early 60's with the initials BH. He was probably in his twenties or thirties."

"Geez. So he'd be like in his 80s now?"

I frowned. "I guess."

"Ah." She sighed. "Well, I'll have to do some digging. I'll get back to you." Then she pointed her spoon at me. "And then you will tell me the whole story, right?

"Of course. As soon as I can."

We finished up and I went back to work.

When I got home after work, Dee was waiting at my kitchen table. I looked at her quizzically.

" There is no way you got that information that quickly."

" I did not, I just wanted to come by and talk with you." She smiled. "The diner has ears."

There was a tone to her voice that I didn't recognize. "Is there something you want to share with me? Are you okay?"

"I'm fine, I guess I've just been taking stock of things lately. It's really weird being an empty-nester. And it's really weird to be at the school without one of my boys there. Is this a midlife crisis?"

I reached across the table and took my best friend's hand.

"For the past 19 years you have been a full-time wife, a full-time teacher, a full-time mother, and my full-time best friend. Honestly any two of those would be enough to break a normal woman." I sighed. "But you are extraordinary. Now you're looking for the next thing to be brilliant at and I have every confidence that you'll figure it out."

She lifted her eyes to mine and they glistened. She leaned over and kissed my cheek and said, "I don't want you to think that I regret a thing. I wouldn't have wanted it to be any other way." She pushed up from the table. "I should get going. Mark and I are going out to dinner."

"Ah, that's nice." I paused. "But New York was great, right?"

She shrugged. "It was good." She grinned. "I guess I'm used to a slower pace these days. One thing about New York is that it's on 24/7, busy, hectic, noisy. But it sure was an experience. Travel can be tiring, that's all."

What had brought this on? I understood the empty nest syndrome. When Zoey went to college, the house had been incredibly empty. I had already lost my Harry. Thank God that Diane had Mark.

I was going to have to think about some volunteer activities that might expend some of Diane's energy and fill her time. This took "going through the change" to a whole new level.

I called the Library to check up on the preparation for tomorrow's sale. Our senior volunteers had offered to step in so Lucy and I wouldn't have to work into the evening. We let them.

Harry gave me the cold shoulder for a bit but after I let him win at Jeopardy, he relented and let me pet him good night. Sitting up in bed, Gabe and I caught up a bit on anything that had nothing to do with my sisters.

"I told Diane about our mystery man."

His eyebrows rose. "Isn't the quilt business somewhat confidential?"

"Yes. But I just asked her to find a guy with the initials BH who might have moved away in the '60s."

"Sounds like quite a challenge."

"Well, you know Diane. And maybe it will distract her from whatever ails her. She's acting weird."

Gabe shoved over to my side. "Speaking of distractions…"

Suddenly it seemed like a long time since I had felt those strong arms around me. I admit I'm a sucker for that. Isn't everyone?

Skipping blithely ahead to the morning, I woke to realize with both joy and trepidation that it was Saturday. I don't normally work Saturdays but we had the book sale starting at 10. But I didn't need to rush to get up.

The sun came in warm and I watched it wave back and forth across the room. Gabe was up and gone. He had always been an early bird and somehow semi-retirement hadn't changed that.

I found coffee and a fresh croissant in the kitchen. The man knows me so well. They do say that the way to a woman's heart is through her stomach, right?

By the time I got there, we had half an hour until opening but there was a line down the steps. I scooted around to the side door. I found Lucy and two volunteers inside. We quickly decided that I would oversee the process and help anyone who needed it while keeping an eye on things. I'm not going to name names but there might be a couple of folks in town who would try to leave without paying.

Lucy was on the cash box with Vivien assisting and Grace would hand out the bags as people came through the front doors.

Our Friday evening seniors social group had put the tables up and put the boxes on top and underneath for our customers to sort through. They were divided into fiction (two tables), non-fiction (one table) and children's (one table) with one more table for miscellaneous (travel, self-help and so on). Thankfully, they had all done it before and it was just fine.

I raced into the kitchen/break room and made coffee for everyone. Lucy, always the thoughtful one, had picked up donuts and muffins. We had 15 minutes to fortify ourselves.

As a courtesy, we opened five minutes early to the people waiting outside.

You'd have thought it was a department store at five am on black Friday the way they pushed through those open doors.

Twelve

"How did it go?"

I laughed. "Like wildfire. It does my heart good to see that people still want books. On the other hand, it was like a fire sale. I had to break up a couple of fights!"

Queenie laughed back. "Bodice rippers?"

"Pretty much. Although there were a couple of hot biographies that caused a fuss."

"We missed you at quilt guild."

"I hated missing it. Anything exciting happen?"

"Polly came by and helped with some of the girls' projects. I think she really enjoyed helping Brit with the baby things."

"Uh oh."

Queenie chuckled through the phone. "Que sera sera, my dear."

"Right."

"So are you too tired to finish the notes?"

"I think I'd rather do it tomorrow if that works for you."

"No problem."

"Gabe may be at the wood shop. Why don't we go do a fancy brunch somewhere?"

"I'd love that. Then we can come back to the shop and wrap this project up."

I was quiet for a minute. On the one hand, I would be thrilled to finish reading the notes. On the other hand, then we'd have to decide what to tell Emma.

"I know. It's likely going to be good news, bad news." She sighed, reading my mind yet again. "How about if I pick you up at 11?"

"That's fine. Thanks Queenie."

"'Bye, love."

I was tired but I wasn't sure if it was mental or emotional. The sale had ended at two. It took us another hour to put things in the storeroom and close up. Thankfully, the library was now closed on Sunday. The town folk didn't seem to mind and the Council was thrilled at the cost savings. After the day we'd had, even the volunteers who help at the front desk were glad not to be expected in the next day.

I pulled Gabe out of his garage office and we went for a walk. I needed the fresh air. Then we took a quick nap before having dinner which consisted of an assortment of leftovers. We really never mind it, after all, it's a few bites of food that you already liked the first time around.

We watched a movie. It was a very quiet night and I was glad. I find that I am increasingly aware of the preciousness of ordinary things.

As we lay in bed, my husband's voice filtered through my pillow.

"You're thinking about it, aren't you?"

I was tempted to wise crack, "Thinking about what?" but there was no point, really.

I'm sure he heard me sigh. "It's just that sometimes you find out things you wish you hadn't. And you can't change them."

I felt him nodding. "Are you talking about your family or Emma's there?"

"Both, I guess. But more about Emma's at the moment."

He already knew about Eleanor's pregnancy and the fact that the baby was likely not her husband's. But I told him now about the hitting and how she had warned him not to hit Edna.

"She said she'd kill him in his sleep," I whispered.

"And you think she did?"

"He died a few months later in a quote unquote farm accident."

"But you'll never know for sure."

"We understand that. And neither will Emma."

"Will it matter to her?"

"That's the big question, isn't it? But it only comes up if we tell her, doesn't it?"

Thirteen

There's not much more comforting than a brunch buffet. There's a really good one in the next town down the interstate and neither Queenie nor I needed to ask where we were going. It was busy, as expected, but we chatted with neighbors and had no trouble filling our plates and finding a seat.

My mouth is watering just telling you, not to torture you, that they had chicken and waffles, sausage gravy on biscuit, and fried potatoes with peppers and onions and a whole lot more. I have learned to take a bite or three of each item so as not to miss out.

Afterward, we drove back in silence, digesting happily. But when we pulled up in front of the shop, neither of us rushed to get out of the car.

"Well, come on then, let's get this over with," she said, pulling open her door.

I gamely followed her up the walk.

A car came down the street and stopped. "Hey Queenie, are you open today?" a loud voice called.

Queenie turned. "Jessica Turner, you know very well I'm not."

She pointed. "Then what's she doing here?"

I stayed quiet.

Queenie walked toward the car. "That's none of your business. Now get moving."

The woman huffed. "The nerve. Maybe I should take my business somewhere else."

"Promises, promises."

Queenie was capable of giving as good as she got. I knew that Jessica had been barred from half the businesses in town and Queenie knew that it was a good drive to the next fabric shop.

She turned and we went into the shop. I gave her a smile. "Jessica…"

"Is a pain in the butt. She tries to haggle with me on fabric prices! Some nerve. I'm tempted to tell her not to come back most of the time. As soon as she walks through that door, anyone else who's in here clears straight out."

She shook her head. "Such a miserable creature."

"She sure is."

We moved to the back room and started our task.

"We left off at…"

"12. So 13." I prompted.

"Right."

(13) June 19, 1968. Harold is dead. Poor guy fell off the tractor and it ran him over. And he was all the way in the north field, I guess he would have lived if someone had found him before he bled to death. Damned fool.
I just can't stop smiling.

"She can't believe it. So it was an accident."

Queenie looked up at me with her bright blue eyes and nodded. "That's her story and we're sticking to it."

"Amen." I added, "And Edna was three or so."

(14) January 1, 1969. Happy New Year. It is wonderful to have just the two of us. I don't think I'll ever marry again.

"She didn't, did she?"

"No," Queenie said. "I think she died quite young, actually. Edna was only sixteen, I believe."

"Coffee?"

"Absolutely."

"We went out front to the coffee bar set up we used for our quilt guild meetings and made a couple of quick cups. I have found a hot beverage to not only soothe my headaches from time to time but also to be a comfort in times of stress.

"Let's do the last couple and we'll see where we are."

We settled back in.

(15) June 10, 1981. My Edna, sharp as a whip, is graduating high school. There is a local boy named George who has been after her. I have begged her to leave him be. We can find a way to get her into college.

"Geez, so George and Edna were like high school sweethearts."

"You'd never have known it, would you?"

(16) November 22, 1981. My punishment has come. I am dying. I have to leave my poor girl alone in the world. May God protect her and grant her an easier life than I've had.

(17) I am finishing this quilt for Edna. It is my way of telling her things I never could. I leave it to God whether she will ever find these notes.

"That's it." Queenie said quietly.

"That was a whole life," I answered.

"Not much of one, dead at 36."

"Every life has its secrets. Things we have to decide whether to tell those closest to us. Is it being honest, or passing on burdens so that we might ease our own load? I wonder, do you have the right to ease your guilty conscience at someone else's expense?"

"Wonder no more, my dear, because we now have that decision to make."

"But not today."

"No, not today."

Fourteen

Despite all the information spinning inside my head about my new sister, the decisions to be made, did I dream about my sisters and our lost mother? I did not. I dreamt about Eleanor.

It was after three and Harold hadn't come in for his afternoon break. Eleanor sat at the table in her faded housedress and munched a chocolate chip cookie while she waited. He liked the cookies warm from the oven. She thought about the meatloaf she was going to make for supper. It was his mother's recipe. She touched the bruises; it had to be right this time.

She was excited inside. The kind doctor had given her sleeping tablets. She figured if she mixed two of them in his second beer, he'd be asleep before he hit the bed and he'd leave her alone.

Then it was four. She opened the door to Edna's room. The little girl was reading a book to her doll. "Honey, Daddy's late for his break so I'm just gonna go have a look see. You stay right here now; I'll be right back." She handed Edna a cookie and a glass of milk.

She went outside. He was working in the north field and it was a bit of a walk but once she got up the hill, she could see the tractor. It wasn't moving but it sounded like it was running. Eleanor hurried over. She jumped up and turned the key off and looked around. Then she saw him, face down in the furrow just behind.

How had the damned fool managed to get himself run over? She knelt down and put her hand by his mouth. He was still breathing. She pulled back and sat there for a minute.

Then she brushed the dirt off her jeans and walked back to the house. She went inside and poured herself a cup of coffee. Then she sat at the table and had another cookie with it.

It was almost 4:30. She couldn't wait much longer or it wouldn't make sense that she had missed him at his 3:00 break so she dialed 911 and managed to sound breathless and scared.

Probably took another 20 minutes for the ambulance to come and the EMTs to haul a stretcher out to that field. She was ready when they came back to tell her he was gone. So she burst into tears.

Later, after they were all gone, she couldn't stop smiling. She held her daughter on her lap.

"What's for supper, Mama?"

Eleanor realized it was almost dark out. "Anything you want, honey." She put Edna down and walked over to the counter and tore up the meatloaf recipe. "How about we go to the drive-through burger place outside of town?"

Edna's eyes got big. "Really?" She looked around for her father. After taking the phone off the hook, Eleanor had simply told her Daddy was hurt and had gone to the doctor. "Is it going to be okay with Daddy?"

Eleanor smiled. "It's going to be okay with Daddy."

I woke up in a sweat.

"Are you okay? You've been moaning."

"Eleanor." I managed.

He sighed. "Oh dear." He pushed back the covers. "Want to get up and talk about it?"

I shook my head. "No, go back to sleep, sweetie. It's fine."

He gave me a kiss and rolled over. I lay there, staring at the ceiling.

When we met at the coffee machine a few hours later, he asked me if I wanted to talk about it now. So I did. And my Gabe listened in his quiet listening way and so did Harry, sitting at our feet.

When I was done, he gave me a hug. "I'm not a therapist nor do I play one on TV," he said, "but I love that dream. You want to give Eleanor a softer edge, even if you think she killed her husband. You've made it unplanned, just a situation where a victim takes advantage of an opportunity to end her suffering. You've found a way to understand. That's so you, Miranda, wanting to think the best of everyone."

I looked at him with tears in my eyes. I picked up Harry and he laid a paw on my cheek and said a few comforting words in Catish which sounded remarkably like "what he said" and made Gabe and me laugh.

Fifteen

It didn't occur to me until late in the afternoon that I hadn't heard from Dee. I called but she didn't answer. I texted.

Later in the evening, I got a text back.

"I think I have your answer."

"Do you want to come over?"

"Later."

What was going on? Dee usually raced over with her big news, her Watson to my Sherlock, breaking the case.

"All right."

"Love you."

I didn't hesitate. "Love you."

Odd.

Lucy and I started the week as we usually did, reviewing the weekend, in this case the big success of the sale. My in box always seemed to magically fill between Friday and Monday so I pushed through the easy stuff first.

It had just about slipped my mind after a long day and I was cleaning up supper dishes when Dee knocked quickly and came in through the kitchen door.

"I have good news, you got any treats?"

"No." I said and her face fell. I pulled open the cabinet and pulled out some chocolate chip cookies. Her expression changed immediately. She carefully selected the biggest one and took a seat.

She sighed with contentment. I smiled with relief. This was the Dee that I knew.

"I think your man is Brian Harticutt." She nodded. "You remember Millie mentioning a younger brother who had gone to Canada. The timing is right."

"Wow, Brian Harticutt."

"Now you tell me what this is about."

I frowned. "I really shouldn't sweetie but, seeing as how it's you, we've got some old notes that might seem to indicate that Edna Hammity was actually Brian's daughter, not Harold Hammity's."

Dee was nothing if not quick.

"That would mean that Emma could be related to Millie Harticutt." She paused. "Age-wise, she'd have to be Brian's granddaughter, right? So Millie's great niece? Wow. That could sure change her life."

I nodded. "The thing is that Emma asked Queenie and me to read her mother's notes and decide what to tell her."

She frowned and that little furrow appeared between her eyes. "That's a little bit selfish, isn't it?"

I nodded. "I can't disagree. But that's where we are and now we have to decide what to tell her."

"Right. I don't envy you that." She stood up. "I should go." As she started to get up, Harry appeared.

This is unusual. Harry doesn't like Diane; well, that's strong, I guess, but he has figured out that when Diane shows up, Gabe and I are going out of town. He doesn't like it. I have tried to explain that she comes over lots of times while we're still here but Harry tends to see things one way.

He seemed to be blocking her path and staring at her. She knelt down and stroked his head.

"Hey, big guy, how's tricks?"

He looked at her intently, then lifted a paw and said, "Yeowwwguuuddddd." Or something like that. You good?

She nodded seriously and shook his paw. "All good. Thanks, Harry."

I watched in wonder. "What on earth is this about?"

Dee smiled. "No idea."

I closed the door and sat down. She was keeping something from me so there was definitely something to worry about. I turned to ask Harry but he was gone. Personal interactions are exhausting for him.

Sixteen

Polly was evaluating her choices. Number One, and perhaps best for her, was to kill him. Or could she arrange to have someone else kill him?

She thought it through. What if she told Michael he'd have to break into Millie's and steal the money or some antiques and then she called the police? Or if she shot the intruder because she was scared?

She sighed. If Michael got to the cops or even if his body got taken to the hospital, his identity would come out. Too complicated.

Number Two, ask Millie for the money. The very thought turned her stomach. How on earth could she explain her need for it now and suddenly?

It needed work but held promise. She had been thinking about getting a job. If she told Millie she needed to clear up an old debt, maybe she could pay it back.

It could work. The clock was ticking.

On Wednesday morning, she knocked on Millie's office door.

The older woman smiled and waved her in.

"Good morning, sweetheart."

Polly nodded.

"You look distressed. What's going on?"

Polly found herself unable to speak. Tears filled her eyes. Millie rose from behind the desk and came over to the taller girl. She took her by the arm and guided her into one of the two chairs front of the desk.

"Just spit it out, child."

Polly took a breath. "I need some money—to pay an old debt. I'll pay it back, I promise."

She looked at Millie with watery eyes.

"I've tried to think of another way…"

Millie waved a wrinkled hand at her. "How much?"

"$35,000."

"That's not a small sum."

Tears fell down Polly's cheeks. "I know."

Millie went back to her desk and sat down. She put an elbow on the desk and leaned her chin onto her hand.

"I've been thinking. It's time for you to have a job."

"Okay, I understand. But I'm not really qualified…"

Millie chuckled. "You are for this. We both know that one of these days, I'll be gone. I don't think you're aware of how complicated the Harticutt estate is but I think it's time you found out. So we are going to go visit our accountants and have them start training you to handle it." Her face grew solemn. "I have been caretaker of the fortune so that future generations might have opportunities and to improve our community. I dare to hope that you might yet have children to carry on."

Polly nodded. "I'll do whatever you ask."

Millie smiled. "You're a good girl. Now as to your immediate problem. I will write a check for you to take over to the bank and call over there to make sure they don't give you a hard time. I'm assuming you might need cash?"

Polly nodded. "I can't tell you how sorry I am."

"No matter. You're going to earn it. We can start your salary for the new tasks at $50,000 a year. That way, you can pay back your loan and still have a bit of spending money. Does that work for you?"

Polly smiled through her tears. "It does." She walked over to her the small fragile woman and hugged her, a rare occurrence. "But I want you to live forever."

Millie patted her arm. "You and me both, kiddo."

Polly left the house, went to the bank, and then made the call.

"Meet me at the first truck stop on the interstate headed west," she said without preamble.

"Does this mean you have my money?"

She bristled at the idea that it was "his money" but held her temper. "Yes."

It was almost dusk when she pulled in around the back by the dumpsters. He was already there, leaning against his crap car, smoking a cigarette.

The desire to throttle him or run him down was almost overwhelming. Almost.

Polly took a breath and a drink of water and got out.

The bastard put his hand out. "Let's see it."

She got in his face. "First, I want your word, for whatever it's worth, that you will never come near me or Millie again."

He smirked. "Yeah, yeah, okay."

She pulled out the envelope and he snatched it from her hand.

As he counted the bills, she moved quickly behind him, pulled his head back, and held her blade to his throat.

"This time, I want you to say it. I understand."

He gasped. "Okay, I understand."

She pushed the knife just enough that a trickle of blood ran down his neck. "Good, because if you ever come near me again, I will kill you. Say it."

"If I ever come near you again, you'll kill me."

"Damn straight. Now get out of here." As she pulled the knife away, she whispered, "Just taking care of number one, baby."

She heard his car door open behind her.

"Hey, I'm sorry, okay?" He called.

Polly kept on walking.

As she drove home, she wondered how long it would take for him to be back. God willing, it would be after Millie was gone and beyond being hurt.

Seventeen

The prospect of meeting my other sister was never far from my mind. As the next couple of days went by, I waffled back and forth. I was procrastinating and I don't do that. Finally, I had to just deal with it.

"Hey Merrie."

"Hey Miranda."

"So...I have to say this has been quite a shock. It's taken me a bit to adjust but it would be terribly unfair not to meet Rose if she wants to meet me."

Merrie chucked. "That's quite an equivocation, sister."

"I know. It sounds unkind to me too but I feel just weary, emotionally. Does that make sense?"

"Sure, I feel the same way. But now that I've met her, it's easier than you think."

"Right. I was wondering if the two of you would be willing to plan a trip up to see me here?"

I didn't say it at that moment but a small germ of a thought was taking root in my head.

"Fine with me, I'll get back to you." She paused. "Thanks, Miranda."

I clicked off. I'd done it.

We came to a date that was about three weeks out.

Feeling like I was getting things back under control, I put my nose to the grindstone and finished out the week at work strong. My inbox was almost empty, the accounts were in order, the weekend was planned and under control. Hallellujah!

Eighteen

So I went off to quilt guild with a light heart. I had missed the last two weeks and couldn't wait to catch up.

The girls were all smiles and talking about town news. It was charity week which was perfect. We had a good group to move fast through a quantity of items. Shelby Loggins had come in with Sarah, our oldest quilter and fastest hand quilter, Judy who was mid-skill level like me, Brittany, our petite mom and youngest, who made up in enthusiasm what she lacked in finesse, and me, jack of all trades, had a system.

. Queenie called us to order. "Ladies. Our charity project this week is batches of mini-log cabin coasters for the craft show at the fire hall. Apparently, they sold out fast and were a big hit last time. We had six sets of four last time so we'll need to beat that record.

"I have cut the 1 ½" center squares and 1" strips for you. There are 4 ½ batt squares and backing squares. You know what to do. Let's do this!"

Judy, Queenie, and I settled at the machines. We sewed and then handed them off to Brittany, who flipped them to right side out and whipstitched the opening shut, handed them to Sarah, who deftly hand quilted them. Shelby gave them a quick press and added our tag.

It's not like we're competitive but Judy and I bent over our machines determined to give Queenie, who was by far the fastest sewer, a run for her money.

============

These adorable mini log cabin coasters are fast and easy to make but very popular as gifts. Starting with a 1 1/2" square, you sew regular log cabin rounds from 1" strips. Add a batting square and place your backing fabric face to face with the front piece. Stitch around leaving a gap for turning Flip and turn, sew around the entire square or whipstitch the opening shut. Then machine or handquilt one or two rounds. So easy!

====================

During our break, we had our usual coffee but Queenie had opted for croissants and crullers, a break from our usual donuts. Shelby grinned as Queenie announced that Danny's

Donuts had provided the treats free of charge. The donut shop was run by her aunt and uncle. Although she was engaged in following her passion to become a cosmetologist, she still helped out there during what little free time she had.

Tawny, Shelby's aunt, never said much but we all understood how grateful they she was, especially to Sarah. When the rebellious, angry, overweight teen landed in their household where she and her husband were trying to run the business and raise two small children of their own, they hardly knew how to help her. They tried to integrate her into the family; she saw it as them using her as a free babysitter and counter clerk. A couple of years in and the waters were smoothed.

She was on her way now, living with Sarah as she took classes and worked part-time. We all thanked her for the treats and she said just a few embarrassed words about how thankful she was for everything we had done for her.

Brittany, our impulsive pixie, gave her a hug. We used the time to catch up a bit. Brit's baby was walking and trying to talk; Judy's son had a baseball scholarship to York; Sarah and Shelby were remodeling the living room of the big house. I made a comment on the success of the book sale. Queenie stayed quiet, smiling and nodding.

After a few minutes of happy chat, Queenie put down her cup. "Come on, we have work to do."

We scurried back to it and the next two hours flew by.

"Time!" She called and we threw our hands into the air. She assessed where we were and two almost done pieces were quickly finished.

It would have seemed ridiculous to an outsider as we sat in breathless anticipation of the count.

"Eight sets completed!"

Cheers went up and we slapped palms as if we had just won the big game. If you're a quilter, you know.

As everyone was leaving, Queenie came up beside me and asked me to stay behind. I sighed.

When we were alone, she smiled down at me. "Honey, we need to finish the business with the notes."

I felt my eyes widen. That was one thing that I had been able to put completely out of my mind. That voice in my head that chastises me when I lean toward the selfish side whispered, "too busy thinking about yourself, you."

"Okay. What's our next step?"

Her shoulders relaxed in relief. "We need to go see Millie, I think."

Nineteen

"Miranda...and Queenie. Please come in." Polly opened the door and we saw Millie sitting in the living room waiting for us. She nodded us to sit.

"Thank you, Millie. We're here to see you, actually, about a family matter."

"Oh my, are you sure you won't have a bite to eat?"

We shook our heads. This meeting was one of those things we wanted to put behind us, especially as we couldn't be sure how our news would be received.

Polly brought in glasses of lemonade and a plate of cookies. She started to leave the room but I stopped her.

"If Millie doesn't mind, Polly, I think you should stay."

Her eyes widened but she took a seat.

Looking at Millie, I started. "As a quilter, I think you'll appreciate this. Edna Hammity, who passed recently, left behind a lot of quilts."

She nodded and smiled at Queenie. "Which I understand you snapped up."

Queenie nodded back, not the least nonplussed. "I did. And they are wonderful. But there was one special quilt.'

We went on to explain Eleanor's situation and the notes she had left for her daughter, who had unfortunately never found them. She was impressed that we had taken on the task of reading them for Emma.

"My goodness, she seems to have put a burden on you, don't you think?"

"More than you know. She not only asked us to read the notes, she asked us to decide whether or how much to tell her of what was in them."

Polly's eyes widened. "Like, wow."

I nodded. "Exactly."

Millie's sharp eyes were on Queenie's. "So there must have been something in those notes to do with me or, I should say, us."

Queenie replied, "So the notes indicated that Eleanor got pregnant by a local man within her marriage. Her husband thought the child was his. She referred to the real father only by the initials BH. Our local research for someone who was the right age and left town about the time that Eleanor was pregnant…"

Millie caught on quickly. "Brian."

"We think so."

"I can't believe it. For so long, I have no family and now you think I might have another great niece?"

"We've made that guess. There would, of course, be one way to prove it--with a DNA test."

She looked at Polly who had remained silent. "Oh honey, can you imagine? You might have a cousin, right here."

Polly took a breath and struggled to keep a polite look on her face. "Excuse me." She jumped up and left the room.

I was well aware that the woman had spent most of her life struggling to make ends meet. Before she came to Cutler, it was a hard go. One of my concerns had been that she might resent sharing the wealth, so to speak. She had already agreed with her aunt to donate 50 acres of land to the town. But I understood that there might always be that fear of not having enough. Lord knows how many times you hear about heirs fighting or even trying to get rid of each other, one way or another. It's the stuff movies are made of, isn't it? So I watched her reaction carefully. It wasn't good.

Millie sighed. "It is sometimes hard to make a child feel safe. There is enough to share here. I will talk to her, don't worry." Then she added, "So it would seem our next step is to meet the girl."

Queenie and I sighed with relief in unison.

"Great." I stood and Queenie rose with me. "We won't take up any more of your time. We have to break the news to Emma and then we'll see if she wants to meet you as well."

We said our goodbyes. I had no doubt there would be further conversation between Millie and Polly.

Back at Queenie's shop, another conversation took place.

"I think we're doing the right thing, telling Millie and Emma about the connection. When you're honest about it, anyone who might have been hurt by the revelation about Edna is gone."

"Agreed."

I looked at Queenie and she grinned. Then she called Emma, told her we had read the notes, and asked her to come pick up her quilt.

The three of us sat around the shop table.

"It's sort of a good news/bad news situation." Queenie began.

Emma laughed. "Okay, hit me with it. Bad news first."

I took a breath. "It seems that your grandmother had an affair while she was married. The result of that was your mother."

"Wow, you really did hit me with it. Are you saying that Grandpa Harmon was not Mom's father? He died when she was little but I've seen pictures. Are you sure?"

"Well, we haven't run lab tests but your mother seemed pretty sure."

"So I am part of a different family on my maternal grandfather's side?"

We both nodded.

"Did the notes say who Mom's father was?" She almost whispered.

"No, she didn't. But she dropped a couple of hints and we've looked into it and think we might have an idea."

Queenie looked at me.

"As a matter of fact," I took up the story, "we have spoken to this family and they are willing to entertain the idea that we're right. If you are interested in pursuing that, they would agree to DNA tests to prove it."

Emma laid a hand on her chest. "Don't keep me in suspense. Who is it?"

Queenie smiled. "That's the good news. We think that your mother was the child of Brian Harticutt, Millie's brother. He moved to Canada before your mother was born and never knew she existed."

"Harticutt?" She was stunned.

"Yes. We took the liberty of speaking to Millie so she could adjust to the ...shock of having another great niece. A DNA test might be in order, of course. But she said she'd be happy to meet you if you want to meet her."

"Ohmigod, Harticutt. But they're rich!"

We laughed. "They sure are. So you might want to pursue that angle."

Emma clapped her hands together, then sobered as she thought it through. "Since neither my grandmother nor either one of my grandfathers is still around, no one will be hurt if I do. I know my Dad won't care. He'll probably be happy for me."

Queenie gathered up the quilt and put it into a quilt box and handed her the envelope with the quilt notes in it.

"Here they are if you want to read them."

"Maybe some day."

We could see that she was already focused on becoming a Harticutt so we sent her on her way with a big smile on her face and Millie's phone number. While she had never said anything about how she was doing in California, the state of her little car didn't scream success.

Queenie and I grabbed a coffee and took a break.

At almost the same time, we both said, "Polly..."

"I know," I finished. "Millie's probably right. She's been so insecure and uncared for and now she's the sole focus of Millie's attention."

"And fortune," Queenie added thoughtfully.

Polly threw herself on her bed and cried. It wasn't fair. She fought off one challenge and here came another. She pounded her pillow. She tried to take deep breaths and calm herself. Millie would think she'd totally lost it. It hit her that she sounded like her father, whining that his father hadn't done enough, or, God forbid, Michael.

There was a knock at the door. Polly sat up and wiped her face with her hands.

"Come in."

Millie came in and sat down on the bed. "I do try to be mindful of where you have come from, I really do, Polly. But it's hard to see why you think this girl might be a threat to you."

"You don't understand!" Polly cried.

Millie looked at the girl intently. "Am I right in thinking that maybe this has something to do with the money you needed?"

Polly nodded. "I should just tell you the truth. Then you'd understand."

Millie stood. "No, you shouldn't. I don't want to know. I will give you the phone number for Father James at St. Barnabas and the phone number for Adam Melton, a friend who is an excellent therapist. If you feel the need to unburden yourself, do it with them.

Polly stared at her.

"Sometimes we want to tell the truth to unburden ourselves, share the weight as it were. It does us no good and harms the person we share it with. Now it becomes their truth to wear as well." She shook her head. "I'm too old to share your burdens.

"Polly, we'll be fine. That's all you need to know. We will meet this girl and see what she needs from us. That's all. You will have enough, while I live and after that. I have seen to it."

She put a hand under Polly's chin. "Now wash your face and come down to dinner. When this new family member shows up and if she proves to be one of us, make me proud of you."

Polly took a breath. "Okay."

"That's my girl."

Twenty

The time passed quickly but I was glad for the extra time to pull myself together for my sisters' visit. When we heard the car door, Gabe looked at me. I heard him mentally asking me if I was okay, ready to face them. I nodded.

He answered the door and brought them into the living room. I stood up and turned around to face the two mirror images. Then my eyes filled and I opened my arms.

We stood there in a three-way hug for several minutes, then we all laughed self-consciously and pulled back. I took another minute to look Rose up and down. While Merrie was the lean one, Rose was a bit on the chunky side, more like me, really. I have to admit I've never focused on having a model-like figure. She walked with a slight limp.

Gabe, always my hero, brought them drinks and a plate of cookies and grapes. As it was late afternoon, we quickly decided to order food for dinner. We were definitely related in our intent to never miss a meal.

Rose sat there with her hands folded in her lap and I drew her out with questions about her childhood, her mother (Jane) and how she felt about having us in her life.

She spoke quietly. "I have always felt as if a piece of me was missing. Sometimes I figured it was just because I don't have a dad. But once I found out," she flushed, "and I saw you, I knew it was because I had sisters. They say that, even if twins or triplets are separated at birth, they still can grow up to be amazingly similar."

We all exchanged looks and laughed out loud, at the same time.

"I think that's possible," Merrie said wryly.

I looked at my watch. "I have a surprise for you two. I hope it's not too soon for another surprise."

Gabe had managed to get the Faceshare screen on our TV and suddenly my daughter's lovely face appeared.

She looked a bit concerned.

"It's okay. Zoey, everything's okay."

She relaxed and smiled.

"I have someone I'd like you to meet."

"Okay, I guess?" She looked concerned.

"Honey, I would like you to meet your Aunt Rose, our missing triplet."

"Get out," she squealed.

Rose moved in front of the camera next to me and smiled.

"Ohmigod. Mom!" Zoey's eyes filled with tears and I saw an arm come into view around her as Michael moved in to support her.

"Hi, Zoey. It's great to meet you," Rose said. "I hear you have the world's most beautiful babies."

Zoey managed a nod. Michael's handsome face moved in front.

"Hi Mom and sisters. While Zoey composes herself, maybe you'd like to meet the kids."

The camera moved and we saw three cribs in a bedroom. He introduced his sons, his voice filled with pride. "This is Harrison Michael, he's okay with Harry. This is Carter Gabriel, he is a bit stodgy and prefers Carter." Then on to the girl. "This is Daisy Diane, we call her DeeDee." I wasn't the only one crying.

Beautiful baby faces, sleeping, came one by one onto the screen. I wanted to hold them so badly it hurt.

Then he moved quietly back into the living room and Zoey, now smiling, came on.

"What do you think of my kids?" She smiled with the same pride we had seen in Michael.

Merrie cleared her throat. "Definitely the most beautiful babies ever."

Rose nodded furiously, wiping her eyes.

We heard a wail in the background, which grew into three.

"Well, I guess naptime is over." Zoey took a breath. "It's amazing that you guys are back together. And now they have two aunts. Three of them and three of you!! We look forward to meeting you in person, Rose. Enjoy your reunion."

And the screen went dark. And yes, all three of us were now grinning.

The next hour passed quickly as we recounted every step of the triplets lives so far. Yes, it was possible to tell the boys apart. Harry had curly brown hair and Carter had the bluest eyes and was just a bit heavier. Deedee had brown eyes and was the smallest. And, of course, Zoey dressed her in pink mostly.

The pizzas came and we had our dinner at the kitchen table. Gabe came and went, giving us space. We had arranged for the sisters to stay at Queenie's. Our ranch had only one guest room and we had decided it would be a push to ask them to share a room. Queenie was, as always, delighted to have company and show off her lovely Victorian. I had often teased her about turning it into a B&B.

So I drove them over and enjoyed the look on Queenie's face when she saw Rose. Rose smiled and said quickly, "It's lovely to meet you. I'd like to say I've heard a lot about you but I haven't...yet." She laughed. "Thank you for putting us up. This house is amazing!"

That certainly broke the ice with Queenie. I left them with her, knowing they were in for a tour and then probably a drink and some nibbly things. I trusted my friend and I like to think that she appreciated that trust. Queenie lived alone but I don't think she planned it that way.

The next day, I came over early and we all had breakfast together. I had taken the day off, not sure exactly how long they were staying.

I gave them a quick tour of the area. Merrie had already seen some of it but Rose was enthralled by the Amish farmer's market. I took them over to Queenie's shop and found that Rose had never been exposed to quilting before! Queenie rose to the challenge and just about got her to promise to take up sewing and quilting. There was no point in arguing with her so I let her have her head.

After we left, I quietly told Rose she didn't have to go along with it.

She grinned. "I know."

I told the others to give it a minute and walked in first. I flashed three fingers at Sylvia. She nodded. I could see the emotions tumbling across her face and then my sisters came in. Her eyes widened and she came straight out.

"Oh dear Lord, there are THREE of you now!" She put a hand to her heart and I introduced her to my sisters. She had met Merrie but Rose was, of course, a bit of a shock and she did actually look more like me.

Sylvia caught her breath. "Okay, then. Three iced teas coming up. Today's specials are meatloaf with cornbread and a Cobb salad with homemade roll."

"Meatloaf for me," Merrie and I said in unison.

"I think I'll try the Cobb," Rose said with a devilish grin.

Sylvia went back to the kitchen, shaking her head.

Twenty One

Millie had a private phone call with Emma and they arranged for her to have a DNA test before coming to the house. She wanted to give Polly a day or two to adjust.

Once the results confirmed Emma as being a Harticutt, Millie invited her over and told Polly to expect it.

Emma came in, subdued but with excited eyes, and they all took a seat.

Millie smiled and introduced Polly. "My brother Brian had a son named Marshall. They're both gone now. Polly is Marshall's daughter. As I understand it, your mother was Brian's child as well but he left town without knowing about her. She was raised by Eleanor and Harold as their own. Edna, whom I knew slightly, never knew she was a Harticutt. But Eleanor left a diary of sorts which alluded to the connection."

Emma nodded. "That's right. One of the quilts that we found when Mom passed had some notes from my grandmother in it which explained the connection."

Millie nodded. "So, we are pleased to welcome you to our little family. As you probably know, it's just Polly and me."

"Thank you." Emma said demurely.

"Tell us about yourself." Polly said politely. "Oh my, have we offered you a drink or perhaps a snack?"

"That would be great."

Polly rose and went to the kitchen, then returned. "Mrs. Bellingham will be right out. Please go ahead."

"Well, I live in LA. I work for an advertising agency." She shrugged. "I'm so far down the totem pole I have to look up to see it. So I do a lot of grunt work: simple design, social media, and such. I do love advertising."

Mrs. B. came out with a tray of iced tea, scones and cookies as well as a few small sandwiches.

They all helped themselves and then Emma continued. Her face lit up as she talked about the non-profits a couple of her friends worked for.

"These non-profits do amazing things for veterans, homeless, orphans. I try to do my bit for them as their advertising budgets are tiny if they exist at all. If I'm being honest, I'd love to create a small agency that consulted with non-profits, making every dollar stretch, getting the most bang for the buck, if you see what I mean. It can make a big difference to their fund-raising."

Millie and Polly exchanged glances.

"It sounds like you intend to go back to LA?" Polly ventured.

Emma laughed. "I sure do. No offense but Cutler's a bit dull. The old "How you gonna keep 'em down on the farm" if you know what I mean. I'm a city girl now. I'm trying to get Dad settled into one of the new condos and get the farm sold on terms he can live with, then I'm out of here."

The relief on Polly's face was palpable. The conversation continued with Polly telling a bit about herself and Millie discussing the general history of the family and the house itself.

After an hour, Millie said, "Girls, I'm afraid I'm going to have to rest now. Polly, you will discuss with Emma what she needs and call the accountants. You know what to do. I'll say goodbye for now, Emma. So happy to meet you, do stay in touch."

Emma rose. "Of course. Thank you so much."

Once Millie had left the room, Polly took charge. "I guess you're wondering what that last bit was about. Come with me." She took Emma into the office and sat down at the desk.

"I have to ask a few questions and they are personal, if you don't mind?"

Emma shook her head. "I've nothing to hide."

"Right. So what is your salary at the agency?"

"Oh, $70,000 plus benefits."

"Right. So we should replace that. And how much would it cost to set up your new agency?"

Emma's eyes widened. "Oh my, I've never thought."

Polly grinned. "I understand. So here's what we'll do. I'll reach out to the accountants and explain the situation. Millie will approve a distribution to you of $70,000 plus $20,000 for benefits, effective immediately. You will draw up a business plan and model for the new agency. Once you have it, get back to me and we'll run the numbers with the accountants and get it moving."

She enjoyed watching the look on Emma's face as she stuttered an overwhelmed thank you.

Polly had a feeling she was going to enjoy this new job.

Upstairs, Millie was, of course, listening in through the air vent and was smiling as she lay down for a rest.

Twenty Two

Three days of visiting and Merrie was ready to go. She said she felt like she needed to get back to the ranch to help her folks. Rose didn't seem as anxious to go and I understood that, too. She didn't have anyone to go back to, really.

She and I stole an hour alone together and had a serious chat. I had talked to Zoey, thought about it seriously and knew what I wanted to say. I had already discussed it with Gabe.

"Rose, I don't know what ties you have back down south. But I've had a sense that there isn't much keeping you there. So now that we have found you, if you would like to move north and be a part of our family here, we'd be glad to have you."

Tears filled her eyes. "Oh, Miranda. I would be so happy to do that. Would I get to see the babies?"

I laughed. "See them, feed them, change them, and, at some point, probably pick them up at pre-school."

She sighed with relief and joy. "I don't know how to thank you."

"Okay, it's settled then. You go back home and settle up whatever. Let us know when you're ready to make the move and we'll work it all out."

Then I approached my final concern. "Rose, please forgive this if it's offensive but does your limp hurt or keep you from physical challenges? We don't want to overdo it if…"

She laughed. "I've been waiting for that question. No, it doesn't hurt. I'm used to it and it doesn't keep me from doing anything I want." She giggled. "Of course, my career as a ballerina took a hit."

I stared at her, uncertain, then laughed back.

"To be clear, I was a small, sickly child. They didn't realize immediately that my hip was dislocated. By the time it was operated on, it was damaged. My ankle was broken, too. Tough delivery, I guess. But the local doctors did what they could. I'm lucky to be walking at all, my Mom said."

She hugged me and I hugged her back.

She then left with Merrie with a smile on her face.

Twenty Three

It felt like Rose pulled up her Southern roots in record time. A quick month later, we were in Newton looking at apartments fairly close by.

We lucked out and she made a quick decision on one with a lot of windows and light. Good choice, I thought. Gabe approved of the security so off she went with the realtor to sign the papers. Gabe and I went back to the house.

When she was done, we all went over to Zoey's.

It had seemed a bit presumptuous to expect Zoey to trust Rose with her babies. We had explained all this to Rose and she understood it might not work out.

But this is what happened. They already had distinct personalities but it was clear that little Deedee was a handful. She didn't like to nap at all and had developed a habit of waking up and howling, waking the other two, who were then cranky for the rest of the day.

She started crying during this much needed naptime and Rose unhesitatingly picked her up and started talking to her, rubbing her back. How did she know to do that? Not a clue. Whether it was the surprise of a new person or she had the touch, the little stinker went back to sleep and she calmly swaddled her and put her back in her crib. Zoey and I exchanged glances.

We went into the kitchen. Zoey put out her hand with a tired grin. "You're hired, Aunt Rose."

Rose started to smile and cry at the same time. I might have choked up a little.

Since she was a librarian like me, after she settled in, she took a part-time job at her local library to supplement her income and pass the time when she wasn't at Zoey's helping out. It was a new life full of hope and possibilities.

I don't like to get ahead of myself but everything in me felt like this was exactly right. Was I a bit jealous? Sure, if I'm being honest. But I have my own rich full life and Rose is entitled to hers.

Speaking of my own life, Dee was still acting a bit peculiar but her energy rebounded and she seemed quite excited and happy most of the time. I told her I have been very concerned especially after our chat, but she just smiled and said everything was gonna be fine so I let it go.

When my phone rang and showed her name, I picked up at once.

I could hear the smile in her voice, " Hey there you!"

"Hey there you yourself. Are you ready to tell me what's going on?

"As a matter of fact, I am. Is there any chance you and Gabe could come over to our house later this evening?"

"You're actually inviting us to dinner? "

"Who said anything about dinner?"

"Well, I guess we could come later."

"Fine, fine, Okay, you can bring dinner. Be here about six."

I was standing there with my phone in my hand in my mouth hanging open when Gabe walked in. I clicked it off and laid it on the table. He grinned.

"Son of a..."

"Diane?"

I nodded numbly.

"We have to be there at six, and we're bringing dinner, don't ask me how that happened."

I heard him laughing all the way to the shower.

On the way to Diane's, Gabe asked if I had any idea of what the news was. I replied that I did not but knowing my bestie, anything was possible.

Mark opened the front door, shook hands with Gabe, and kissed me on the cheek.

"Welcome, welcome!"

He was almost beaming, and his lovely smile and lightness made me feel warm and happy. I relaxed a little. Whatever was going on, it was good.

Diane appeared and went right to Mark's side. He slid his arm around her waist in an easy and familiar motion.

"We brought chef's salad, warm bread, and..."

Diane raised a fit and shouted, "Shoo-fly pie!"

We all laughed. Shoo-fly is a traditional Amish pie with a flaky crust, molasses filling, and a crumble topping. If you know, you know.

"Let's eat and then have pie and coffee in the den." Mark suggested. We all agreed and headed to the kitchen.

We settled into over-sized chairs with cups of tea and coffee and too-large slices of warm pie and whipped cream. After a few yummy noises, Diane cleared her throat and began to speak.

"As you know, I've been feeling out of sorts. The boys being gone, everything just feels different, not really bad different, just unsettled."

She took a deep breath and looked at each one of us. "I guess I haven't felt…needed."

I opened my mouth but she gave me the STOP hand.

"I have decided to retire."

No one moved, then I jumped up and and pounced on her, laughing and crying. I pulled back.

"Wait a darn second! We're the same age!"

Diane smiled and nodded. "Yes we are, Gram. I started teaching right after college, this is my 30th year."

My mouth fell open. "No way."

I noticed Mark was quiet. He caught me staring and met my eyes.

"I think it's wonderful. Don't worry, she will be busy and love it."

Gabe finally spoke. "But how does this make her feel needed and how will she be busier in retirement?"

Mark and Diane exchanged a look and Diane went to the desk. She pulled out a very thick manila envelope and untied the flap. She sat back down and looked straight at me.

"I've been keeping something from you and, frankly, it's been one of the hardest things ever, but I had to be sure."

"Dee, you're scaring me. Please."

She reached into the envelope and pulled out an 8 x 10 photo. Grinning at the image, she turned it toward me and Gabe. It was a photo of an absolutely stunning Asian girl, bright eyes and perfect skin, shiny dark hair and smiling shyly.

I heard Gabe swallow hard.

"This is Mai, and she is our new daughter."

I'm not sure who cried first or hardest, but in a flurry of questions it was Mark who raised his hand.

"Okay, okay. This is something we talked about on and off for years. We have so much, we live so comfortably, in such a safe and free place. It's actually a perfect fit. Girls are not valued in average Chinese families to begin with but Mei's parents died in an accident. She's ten and she's been in a girls school for over a year.

We've zoomed with her and the school officials. We have both been vetted and the boys approve. We don't have the energy to start all over, but we sure have the means, space, and love for this little girl."

Diane moved to him and wrapped him up from behind. I cleared my throat and Gabe put his hand on mine, blinking hard.

"What a lucky little girl."

Meet the authors…

Mary Devlin Lynch lives in the Bronx but spends a few winter months in Florida. She's a notorious multitasker, often working on several quilts at a time, writing two books at the same time, and reading at least one book a week. She also handles the paperwork for her doctor husband's practice, loves tag sales, enjoys a trip to the casino (esp. with her sister), and handles the administrative side of devlinsbooks. Her daughter, Megan, son-in-law Peter, and grandsons, Collin and Luke, live in Natick, Massachusetts.

Beth Devlin-Keune, the youngest Devlin sister, lives in South Florida with her partner of 33 years and four cats. Her Administration of Justice degree from THE Pennsylvania State University, and law enforcement experience gives her special insight into many of our characters. In addition to rooting on the blue and white, she is also a voracious reader, enjoys a trip to the casino, likes a fine single malt, and watches sports and true crime TV.

Other Books by the Devlin Sisters

The Witherspoon Adventures:
Beautiful Disaster (Magee), Book 1
Burnt Roses (Melissa), with Beth Devlin-Keune, Book 2
Before Everafter (Madison), Book 3
Relative Unknown (Cari), Book 4

Cayden and Cat Adventures:
The Wright Move, Book 1
The Wright One, Book 2
The Wright Woman, Book 3

Meredith Abbott Adventures:
Lying for a Living: Meredith Abbott's Adventures in Hollywood, Book 1
Dying for a Headline: Meredith Abbott's Adventures in England, Book 2

A Hollywood Designer Adventure:
Sophie by Design

Skylar Kincaid, Editor:
The Dame in the Diamonds

Sierra Parker, Museum Curator
A Knight in Cairo

Miranda Hathaway Adventures:
 The Quilt Ripper, Book 1
 The Missing Quilter, Book 2
 The Quilt Show Caper, Book 3
 The Quilter's Secret, Book 4
 A Quilt to Die For, Book 5
 The Quilter's Christmas Surprises, Book 6
 The Quilters Push Back, Book 7
 The Quilting Queen, Book 8
 The Quilting Cruise, Book 9
 The Baby Quilt, Book 10
 The Dollhouse Quilt, Book 11
 Candy Quilt Guilt, Book 12

Darcy Garrett Art Shop Mystery
 Stormscapes
 Darcy's Snowscapes
 Irelandscapes

A Fine Mess and A Wedding Dress

Kelly's Teapot Christmas
 A Temptation Teapot Society Cozy Mystery

To Serve the King (a historical novel)
 (Megan Broome Porcaro and Mary Devlin Lynch)

Made in the USA
Las Vegas, NV
14 November 2024